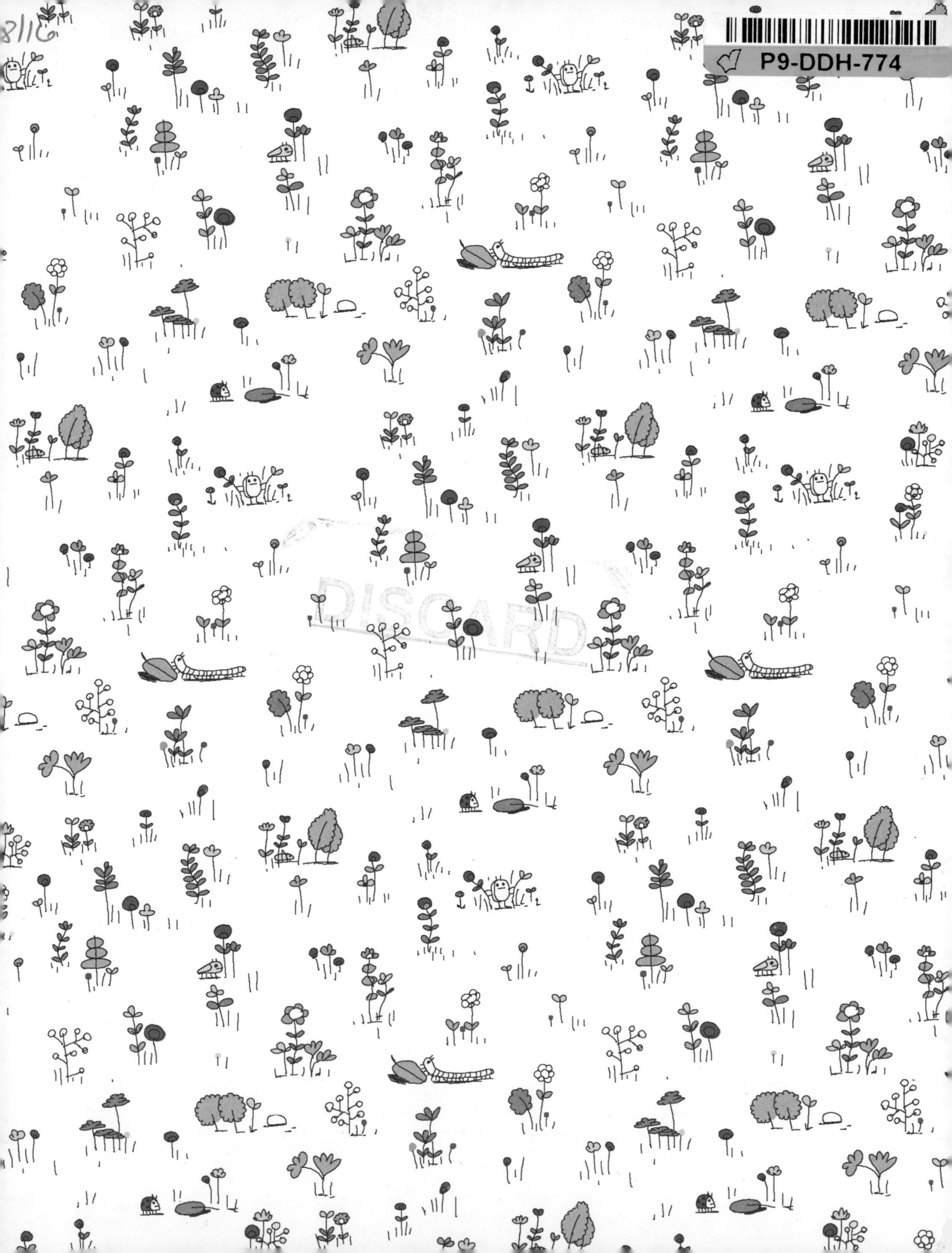

Entire contents © 2013 Anouk Ricard. All rights reserved. No part of this book (except small portions for review purposes) may be reproduced in any form without written permission from Anouk Ricard or Enfant. Enfant is an imprint of Drawn & Quarterly. Originally published in French as *Anna et Froga: Qu'est-ce qu'on fait maintenant?* by Éditions Sarbacane. Translator: Helge Dascher. Translation Editor: John Kadlecek. First Hardcover Edition: April 2013. 10 9 8 7 6 5 4 3 2 1. Printed in Malaysia. Library and Archives Canada Cataloguing in Publication; Ricard, Anouk; Anna and Froga : I dunno, what do you want to do? / Anouk Ricard; [translator, Helge Dascher].Translation of: Anna et Froga: qu'est-ce qu'on fait maintenant? ISBN 978-1-77046-120-8 1. Graphic novels. I. Dascher, Helge, 1965- II. Title. III. Title: I dunno, what do you want to do? PZ7.7.R53Ann 2013   j741.5'944   C2012-907126-9

Liberté • Égalité • Fraternité
RÉPUBLIQUE FRANÇAISE

This work, published as part of grant programs for publication (Acquisition of Rights and Translation), received support from the French Ministry of Foreign and European Affairs and from the Institut français. Cet ouvrage, publié dans le cadre du Programme d'Aide à la Publication (Cession de droits et Traduction), a bénéficié du soutien du Ministère des Affaires étrangères et européennes et de l'Institu français. Drawn & Quarterly acknowledges the financial contribution of the Government of Canada through the Canada Book Fund for our publishing activities and for support of this edition. Published in the US by Drawn & Quarterly, a client publisher of Farrar, Straus & Giroux (18 West 18th Street, New York NY 10011 USA) Published in Canada by Drawn & Quarterly, a client publisher of Raincoast Books (2440 Viking Way, Richmond, BC V6V 1N2 Canada). www.drawnandquarterly.com

Anouk Ricard

ANNA & FROGA

I dunno... what do you want to do?

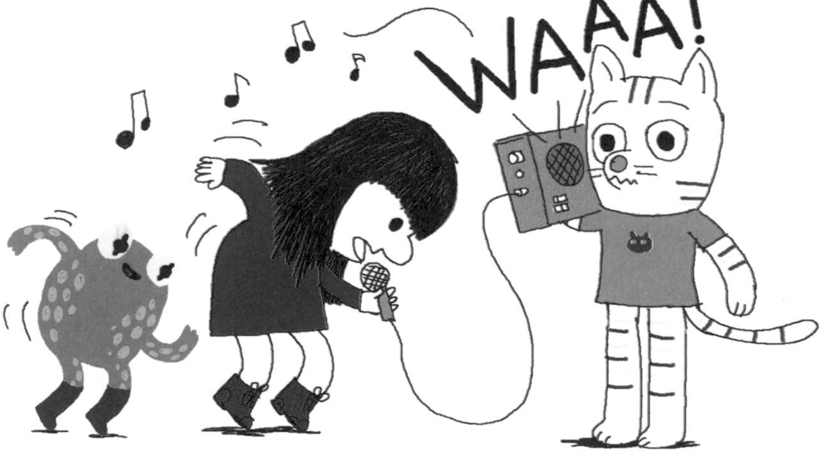
WAAA!

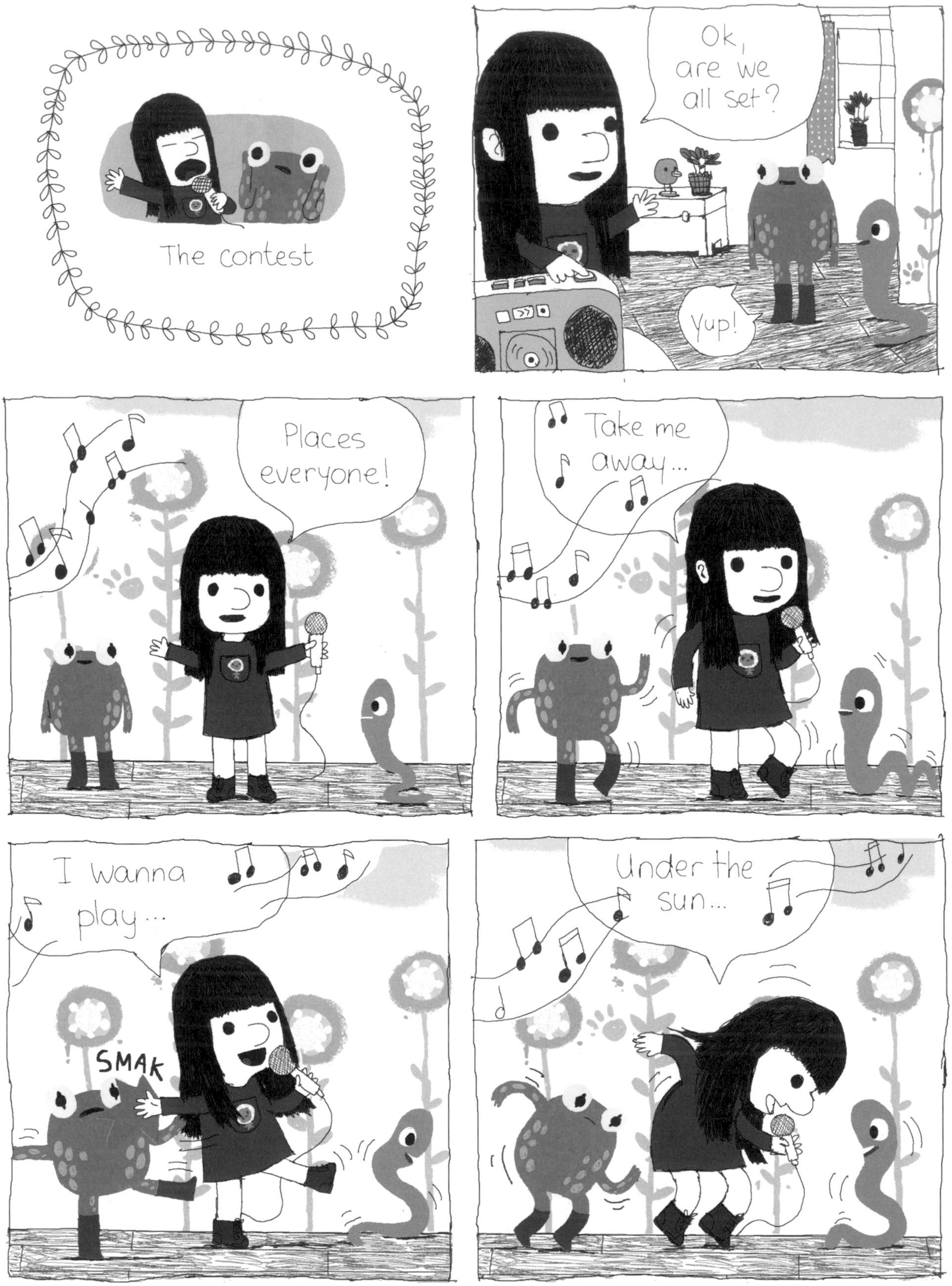
The contest
Ok, are we all set?
Yup!
Places everyone!
Take me away...
I wanna play...
SMAK
Under the sun...

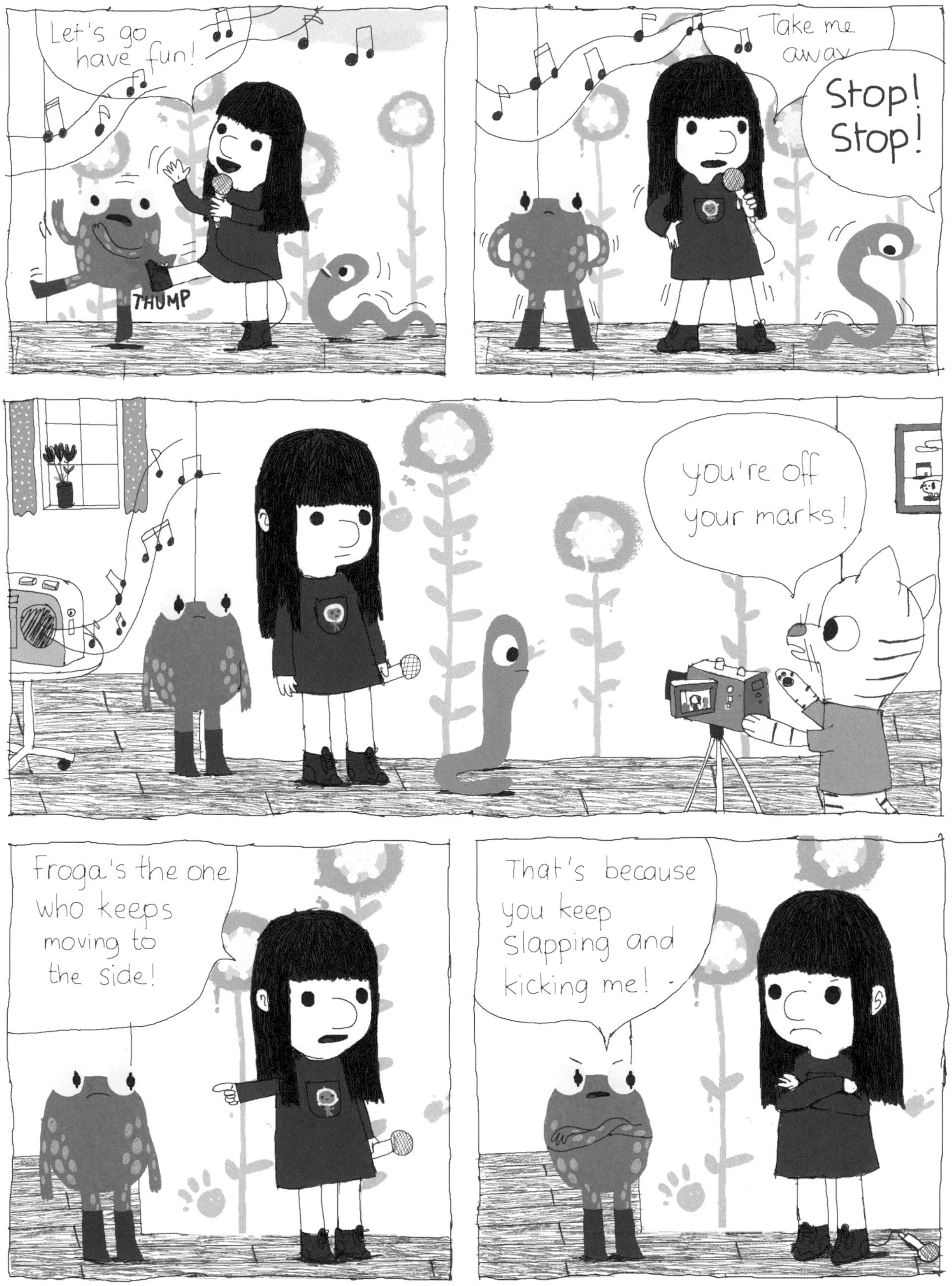
Let's go have fun!
THUMP
Take me away
Stop! Stop!
you're off your marks!
Froga's the one who keeps moving to the side!
That's because you keep slapping and kicking me!

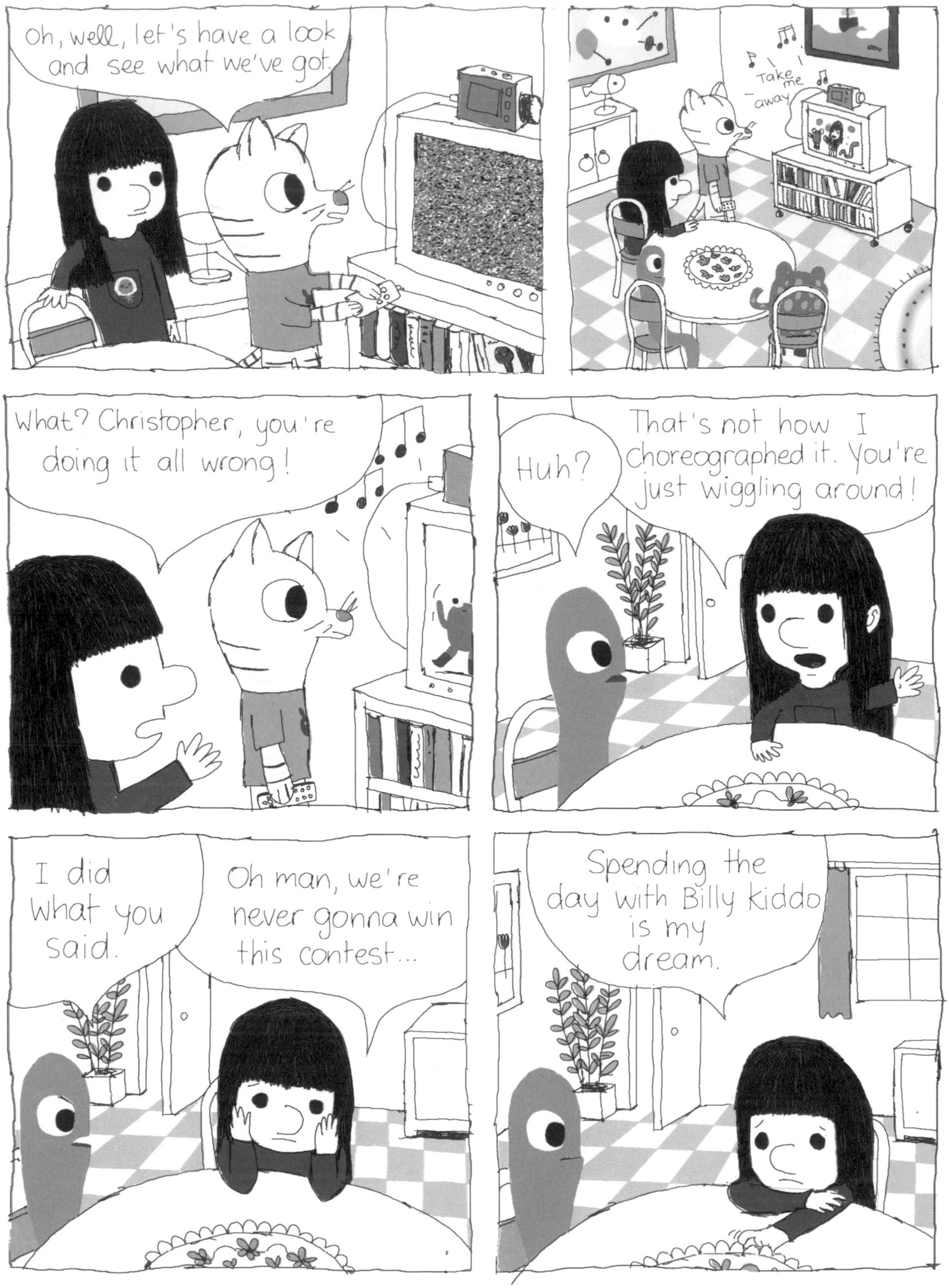

Oh, well, let's have a look and see what we've got.
Take me away
What? Christopher, you're doing it all wrong!
Huh?
That's not how I Choreographed it. You're just wiggling around!
I did what you said.
Oh man, we're never gonna win this contest...
Spending the day with Billy Kiddo is my dream.

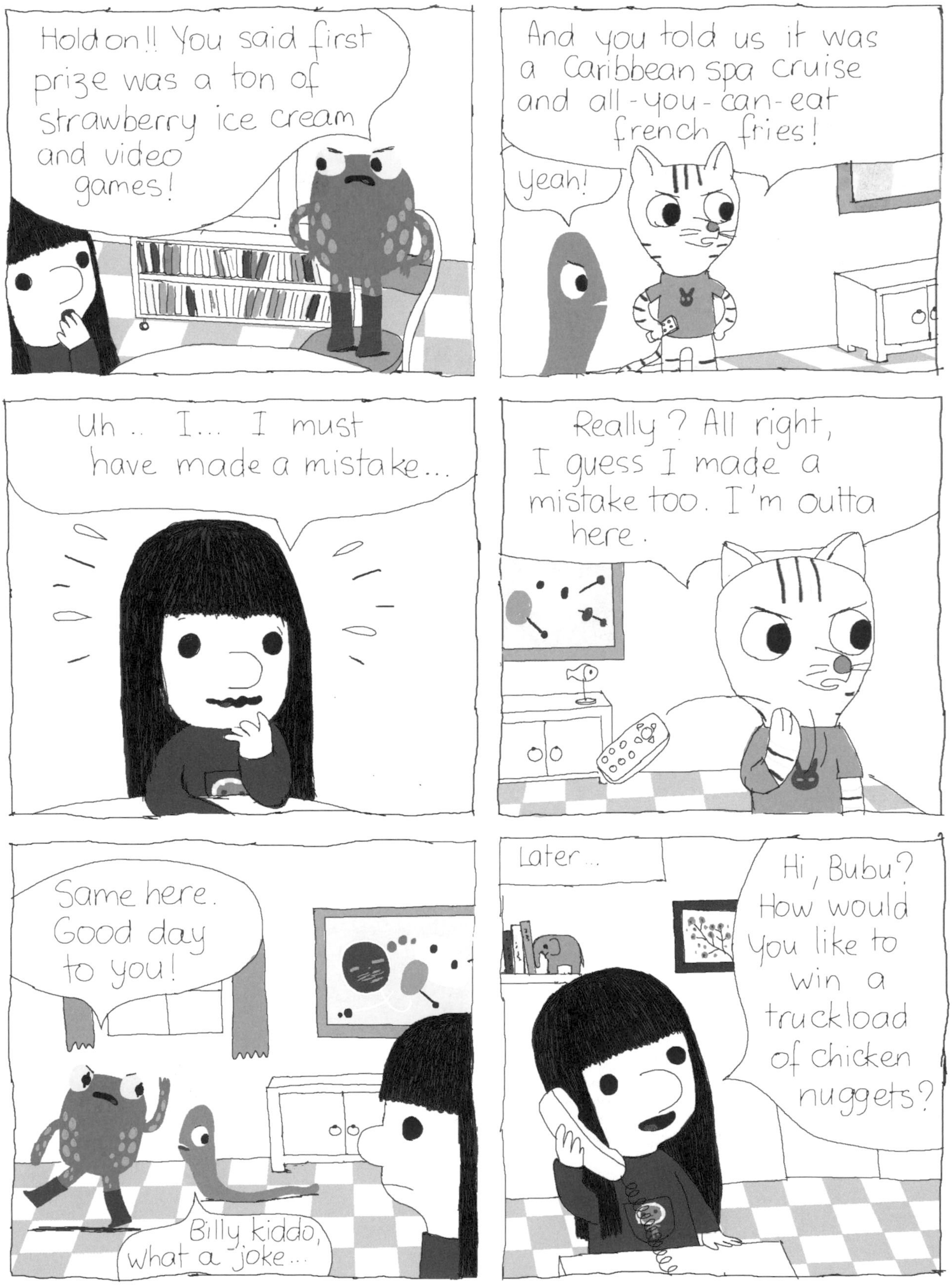
Hold on!! You said first prize was a ton of strawberry ice cream and video games!
And you told us it was a Caribbean spa cruise and all-you-can-eat french fries!
Yeah!
Uh.. I... I must have made a mistake...
Really? All right, I guess I made a mistake too. I'm outta here.
Same here. Good day to you!
Billy kiddo, what a joke...
Later...
Hi, Bubu? How would you like to win a truckload of chicken nuggets?

The moves

The bridge

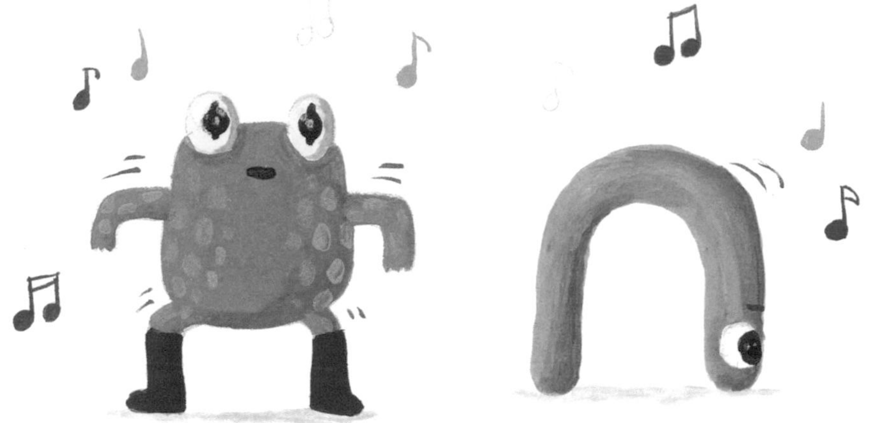

The Skater

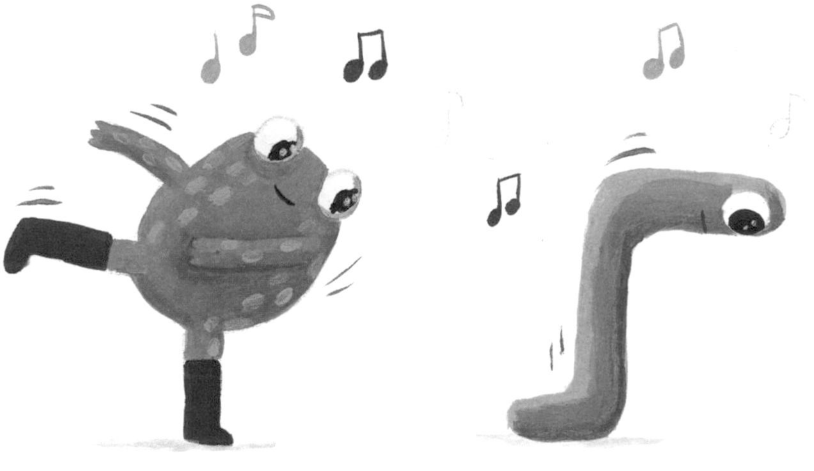

The Eiffel Tower

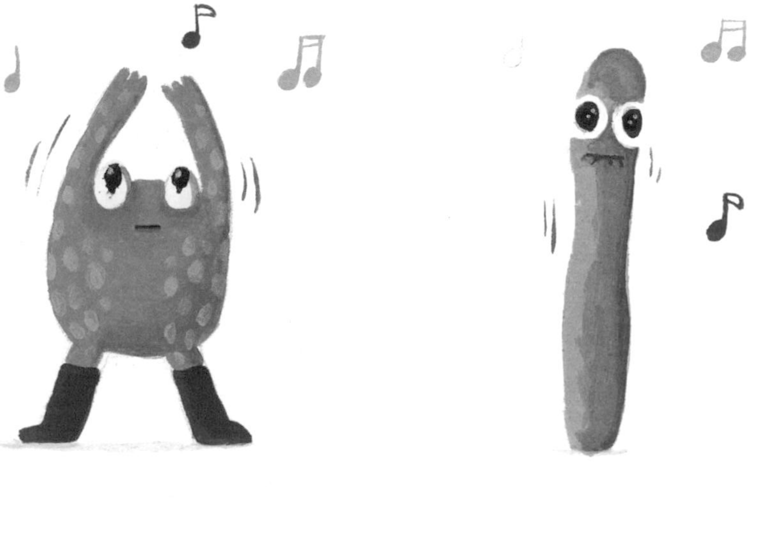

Saturday night

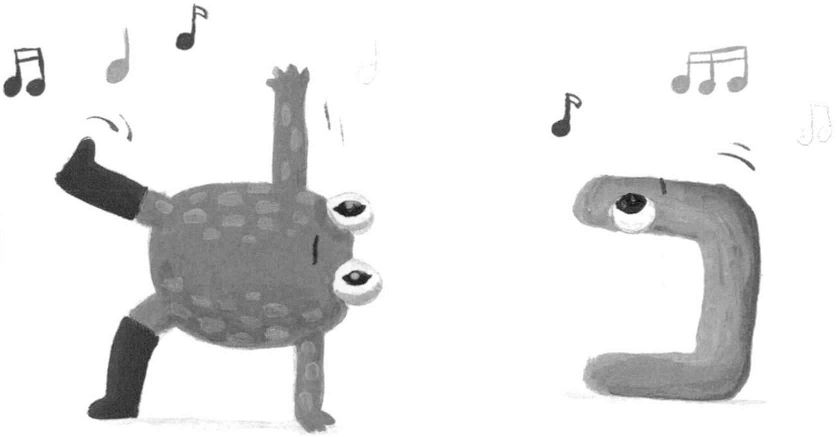

The traffic cop

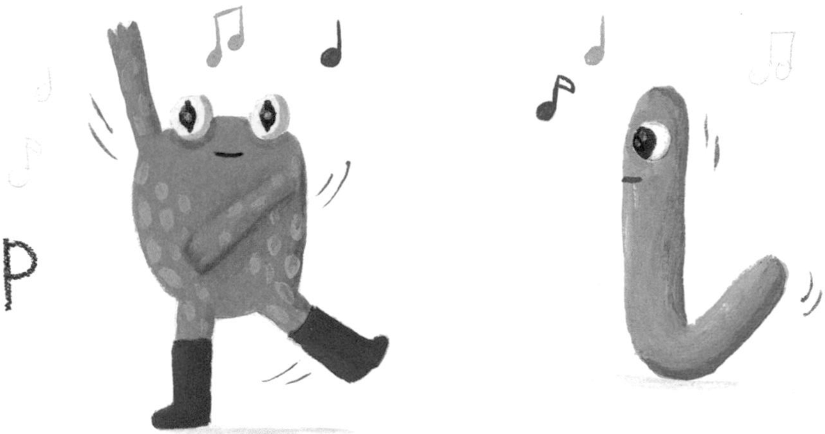

The prima ballerina

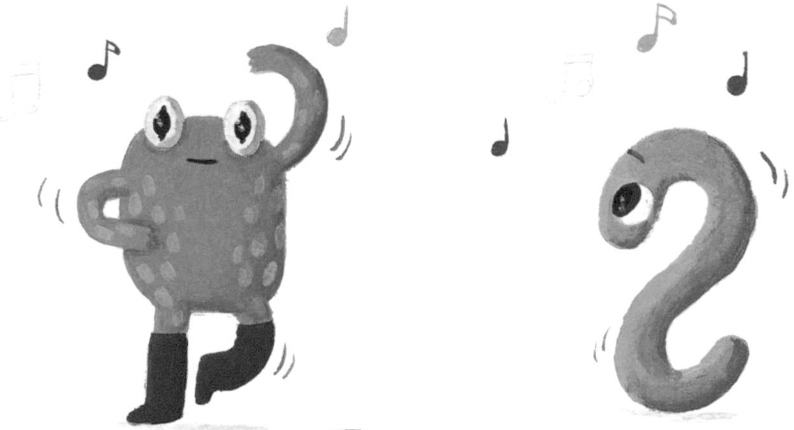

Anything goes (but stay in rhythm)

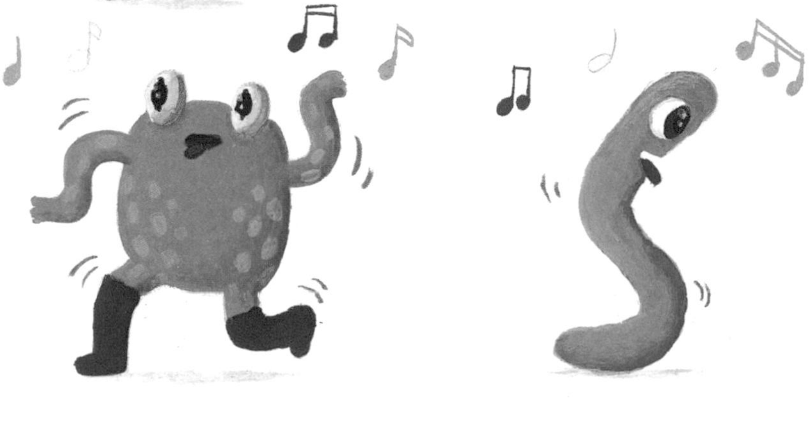

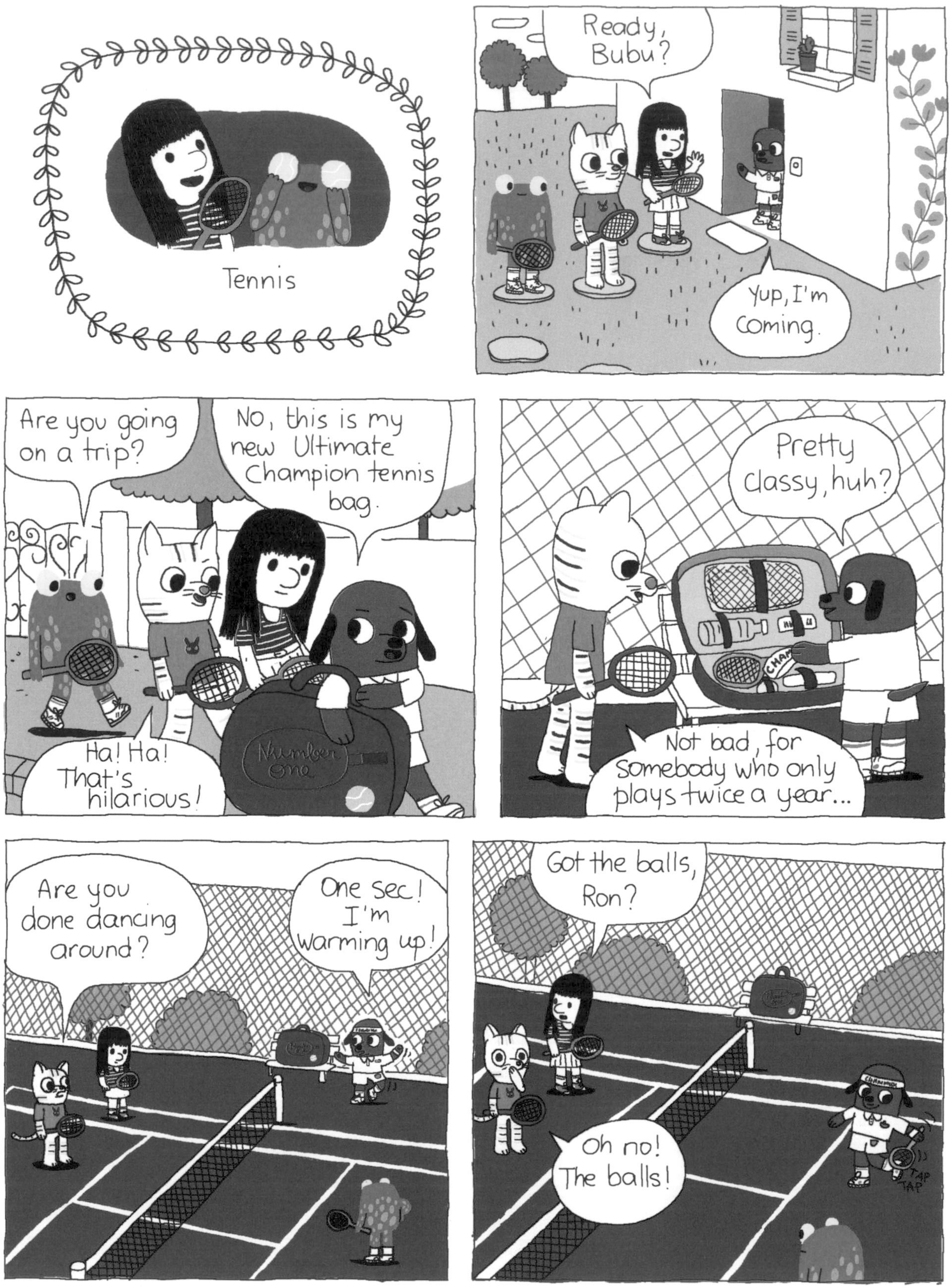
Tennis
Ready, Bubu?
Yup, I'm coming.
Are you going on a trip?
No, this is my new Ultimate Champion tennis bag.
Ha! Ha! That's hilarious!
Number One
Pretty classy, huh?
Not bad, for somebody who only plays twice a year...
Are you done dancing around?
One sec! I'm warming up!
Got the balls, Ron?
Oh no! The balls!
TAP TAP

You have got to be kidding me! Talk about amateurs!
CHAMPION
How about you, champ? Got any balls in that humungous bag?
Of course! I knew I'd be playing with rookies.
CHAMPION
Hey, guys! No arguing! How about you get those balls, Bubu?
Ok, but we need to be careful. I've only got one.
CHAMPION
Go easy, huh? This is pro-level gear.
CHAMPION
CHAMPION
POK
Watch out! Here comes my killer forehand!
GRUNT!
POK

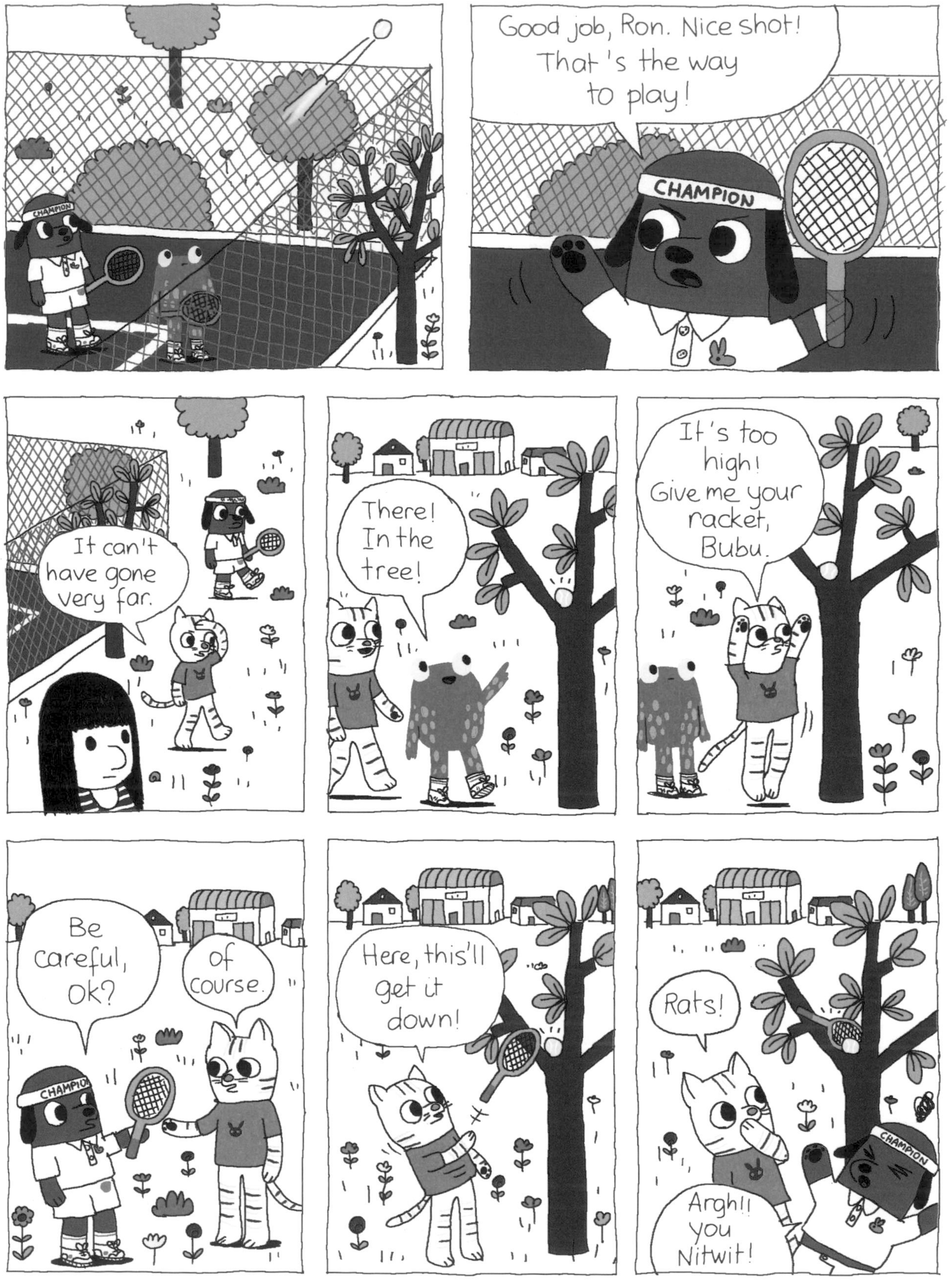

CHAMPION
Good job, Ron. Nice shot! That's the way to play!
CHAMPION
It can't have gone very far.
There! In the tree!
It's too high! Give me your racket, Bubu.
Be careful, Ok?
Of course.
CHAMPION
Here, this'll get it down!
Rats!
CHAMPION
Argh!! you Nitwit!

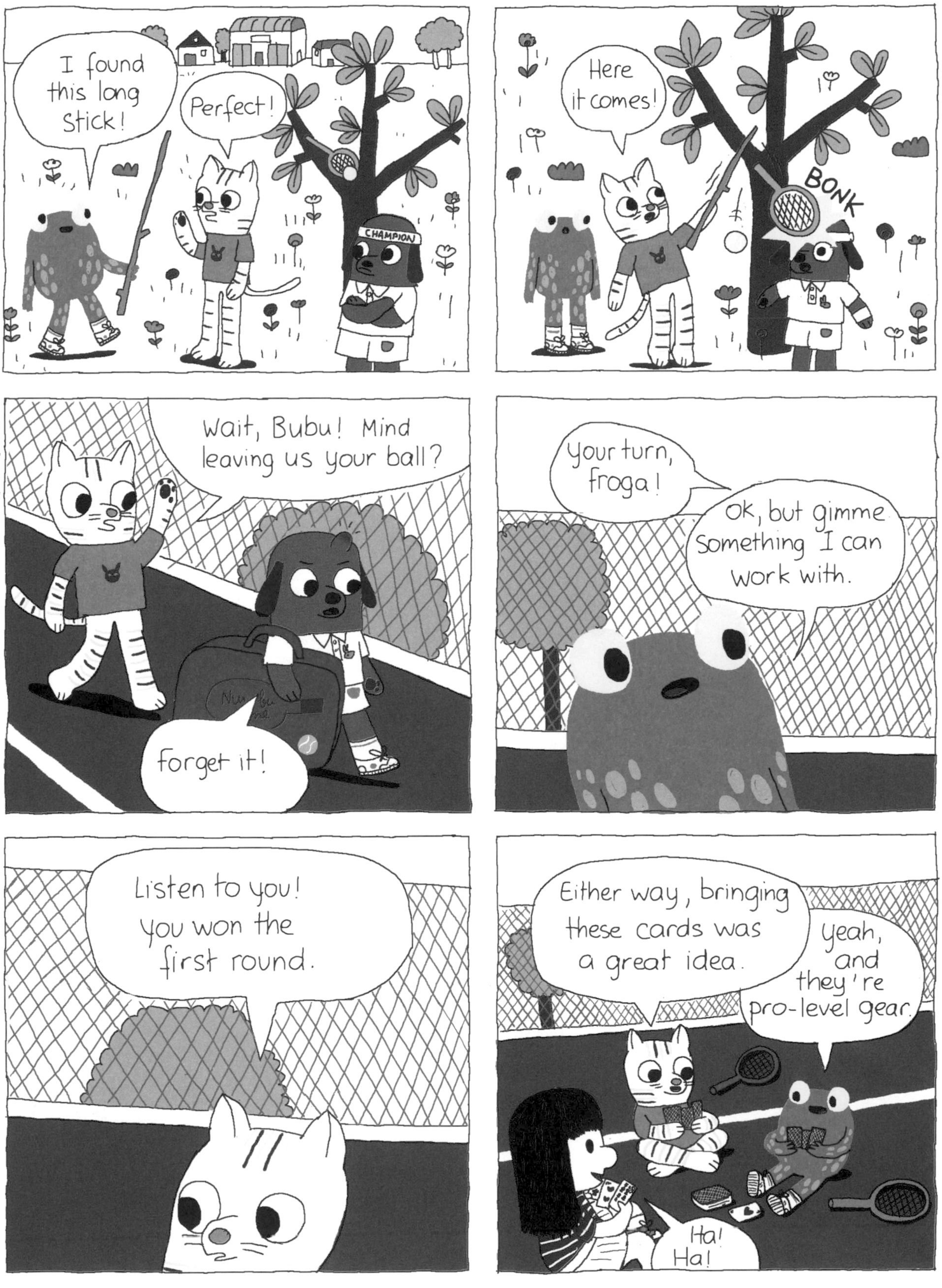
I found this long stick!
Perfect!
CHAMPION
Here it comes!
BONK
Wait, Bubu! Mind leaving us your ball?
Forget it!
Your turn, froga!
Ok, but gimme something I can work with.
Listen to you! You won the first round.
Either way, bringing these cards was a great idea.
Yeah, and they're pro-level gear.
Ha! Ha!

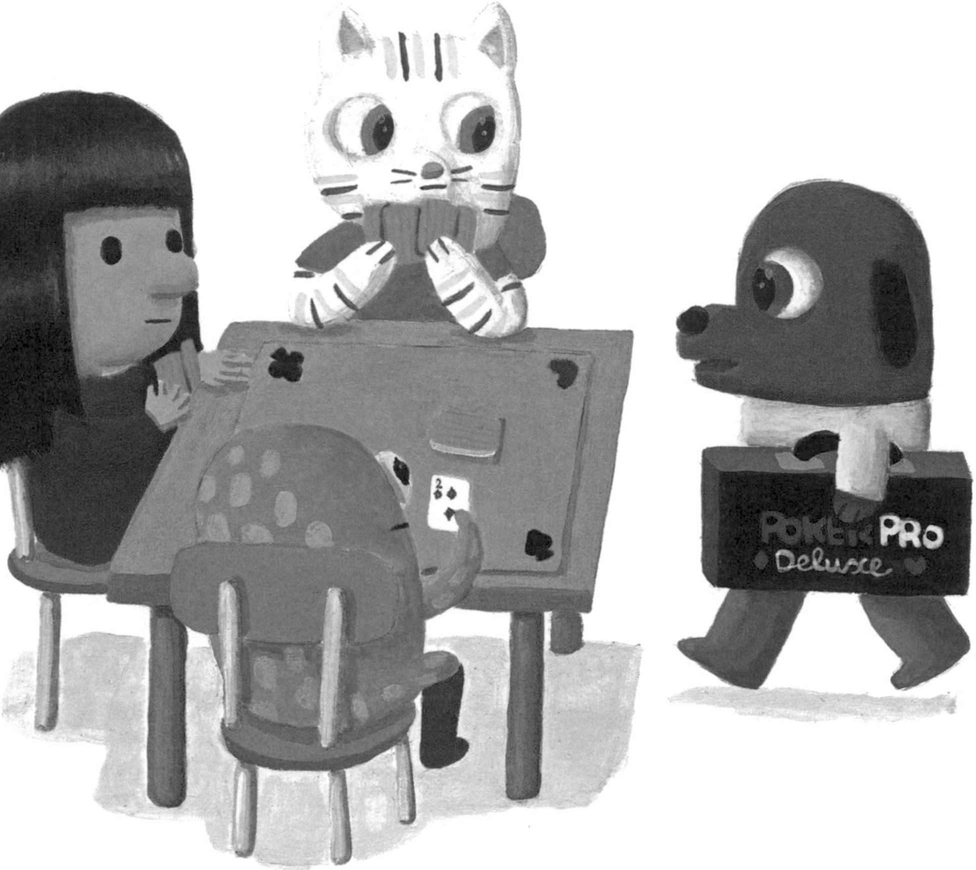
PRO
Deluxe

Hey! Can I play?

I brought my poker set.

Guys, what's wrong? All I said was PLEASE don't bend the cards.

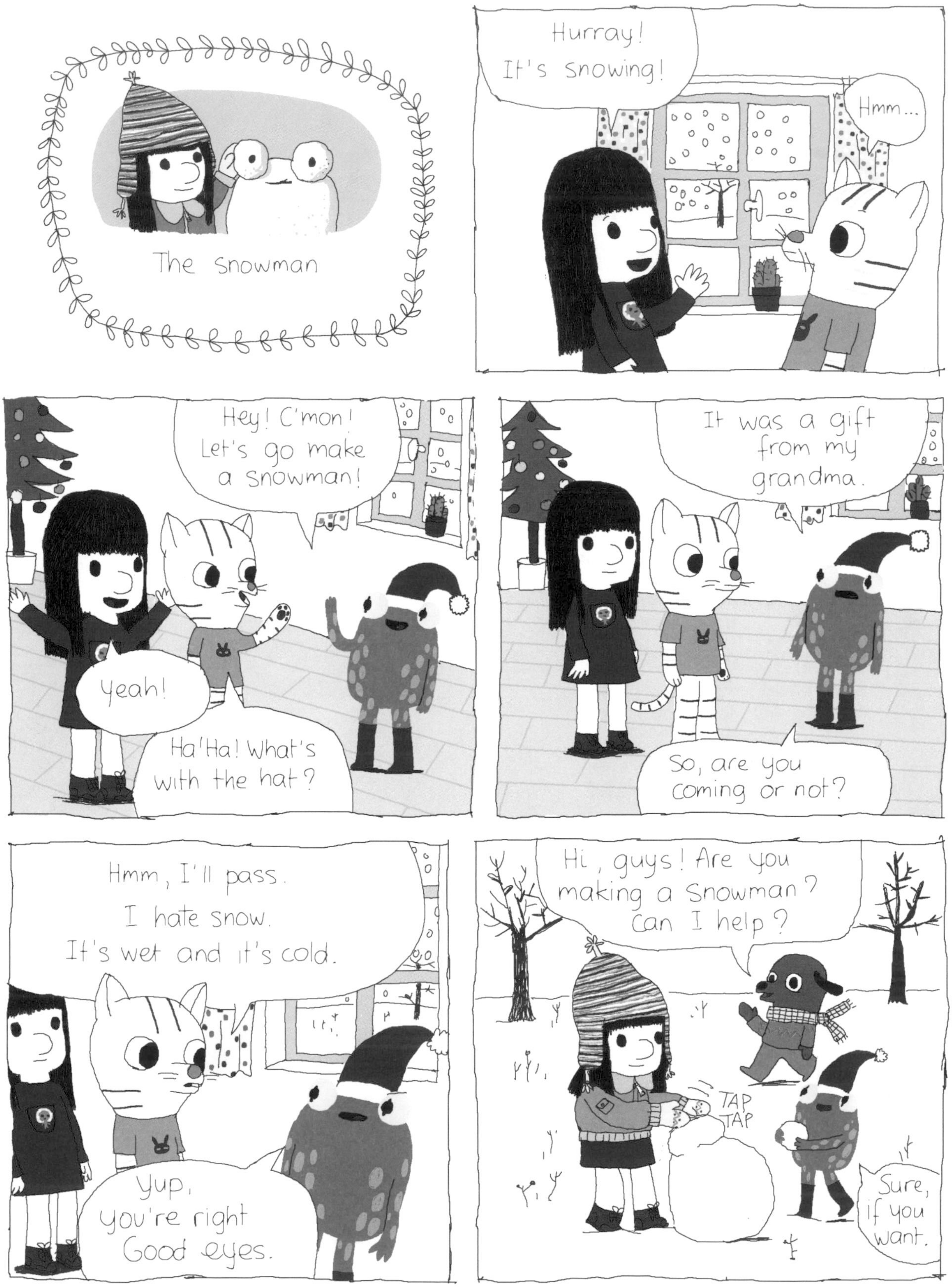
The snowman
Hurray! It's snowing!
Hmm...
Hey! C'mon! Let's go make a snowman!
Yeah!
Ha!Ha! What's with the hat?
It was a gift from my grandma.
So, are you coming or not?
Hmm, I'll pass. I hate snow. It's wet and it's cold.
Yup, you're right Good eyes.
Hi, guys! Are you making a snowman? Can I help?
TAP TAP
Sure, if you want.

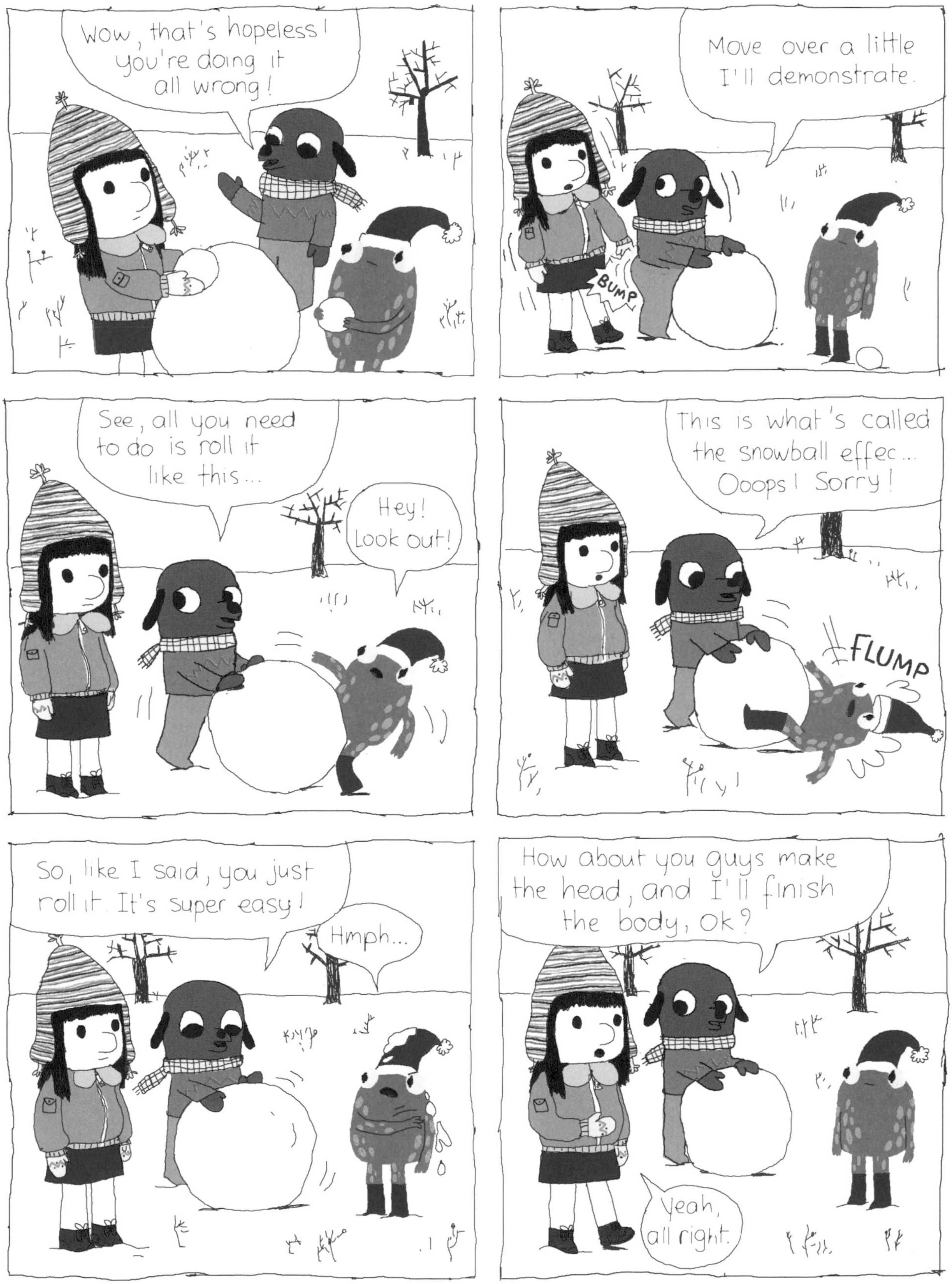
Wow, that's hopeless! you're doing it all wrong!
Move over a little I'll demonstrate.
BUMP
See, all you need to do is roll it like this...
Hey! Look out!
This is what's called the snowball effec... Ooops! Sorry!
FLUMP
So, like I said, you just roll it. It's super easy!
Hmph...
How about you guys make the head, and I'll finish the body, Ok?
Yeah, all right.

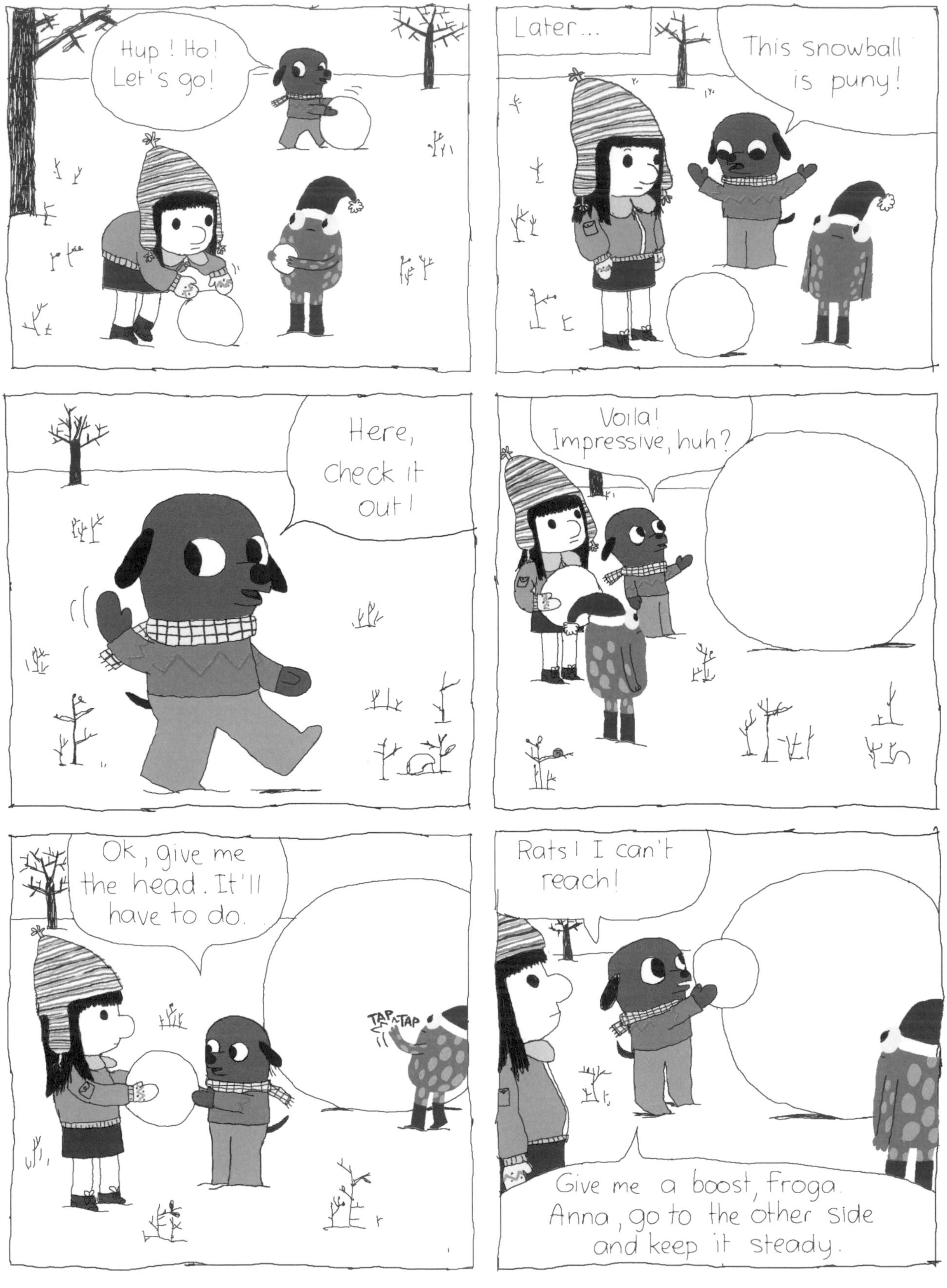
Hup! Ho! Let's go!
Later...
This snowball is puny!
Here, check it out!
Voila! Impressive, huh?
Ok, give me the head. It'll have to do.
TAP TAP
Rats! I can't reach!
Give me a boost, Froga. Anna, go to the other side and keep it steady.

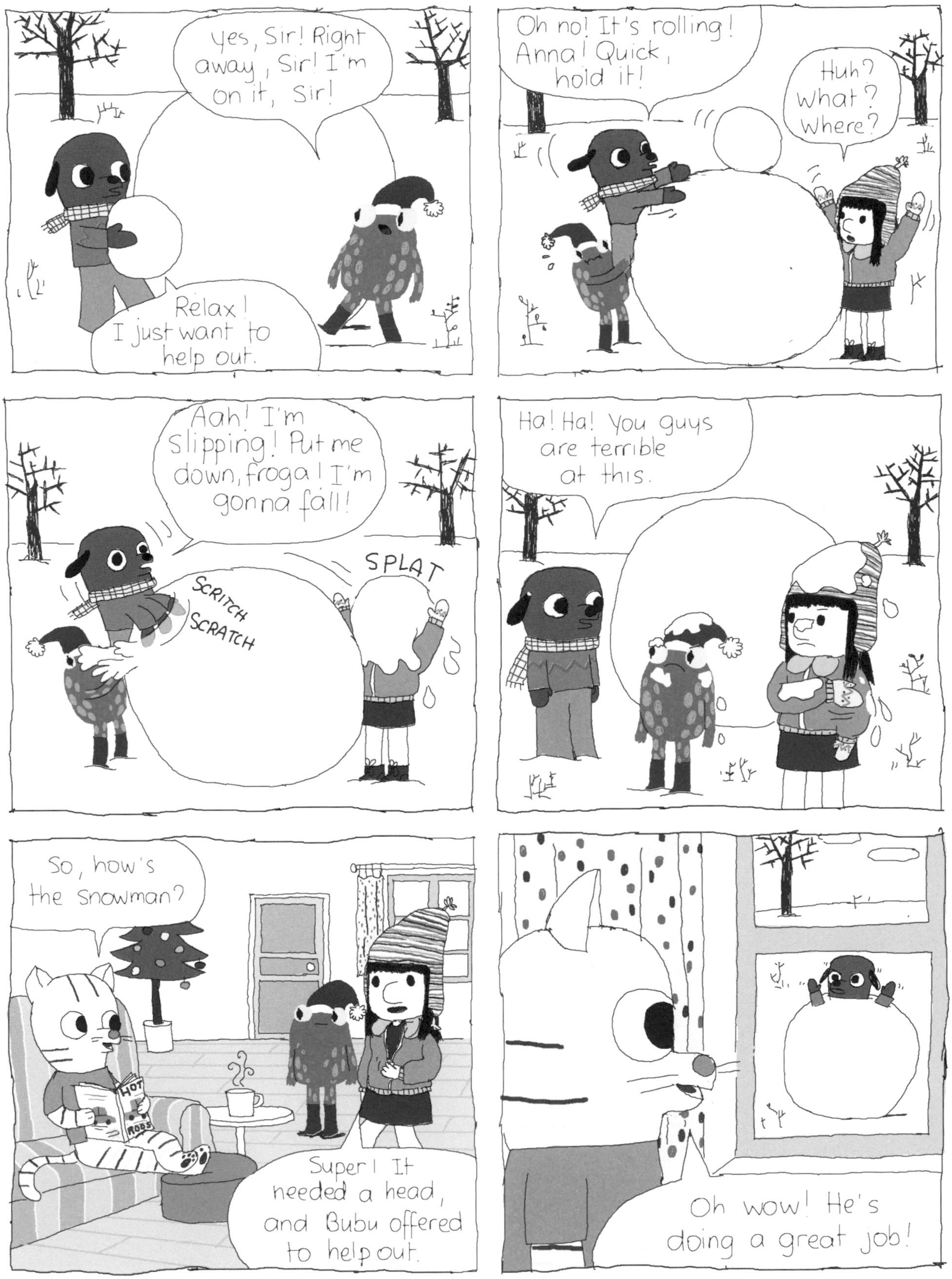
Yes, Sir! Right away, Sir! I'm on it, Sir!
Relax! I just want to help out.
Oh no! It's rolling! Anna! Quick, hold it!
Huh? What? Where?
Aah! I'm slipping! Put me down, froga! I'm gonna fall!
SCRITCH SCRATCH
SPLAT
Ha! Ha! You guys are terrible at this.
So, how's the snowman?
HOT RODS
Super! It needed a head, and Bubu offered to help out.
Oh wow! He's doing a great job!

Ha! Ha! Look at poor Bubu!
Let's go dig him out
He'll be happy to see us!

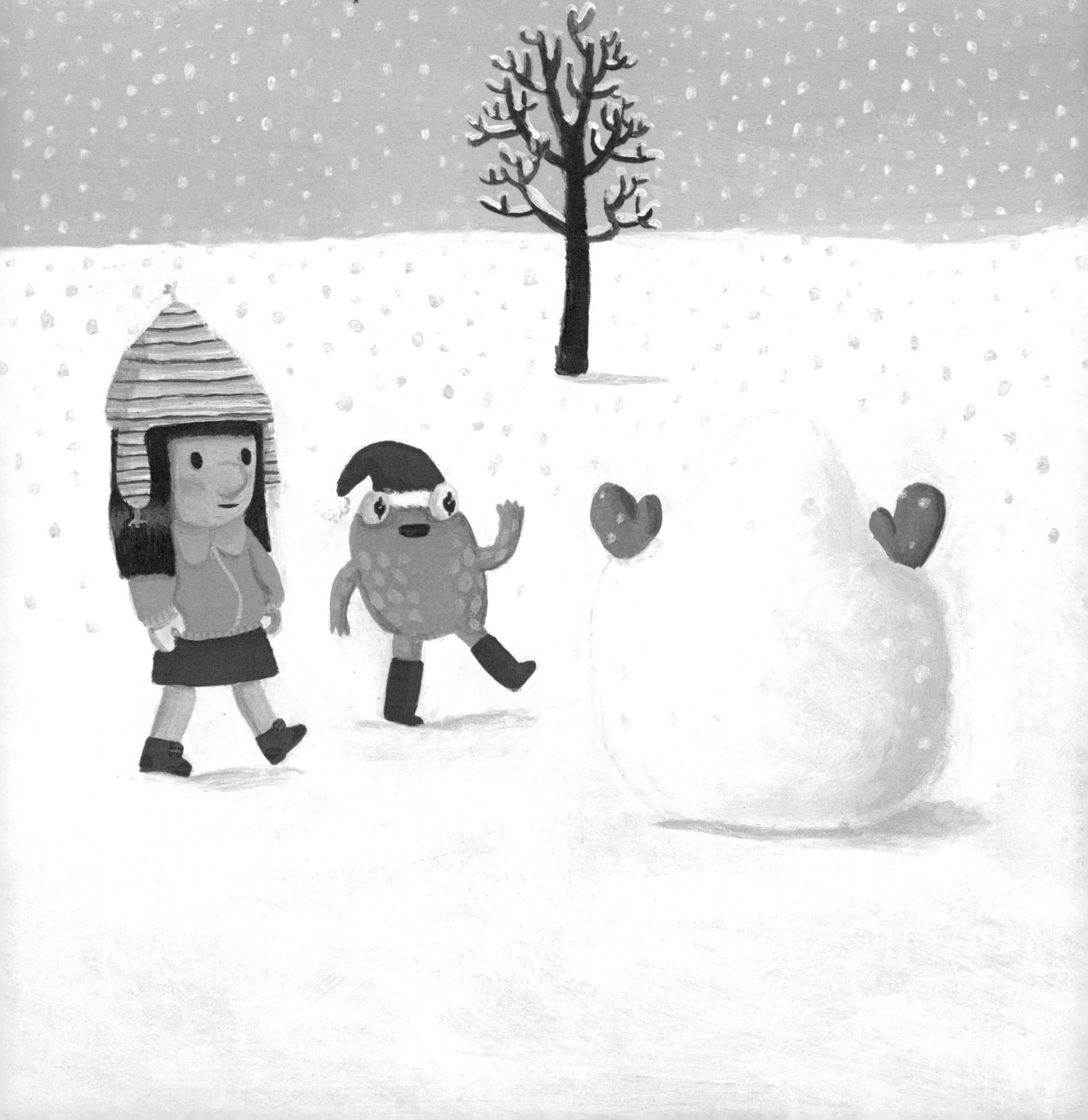

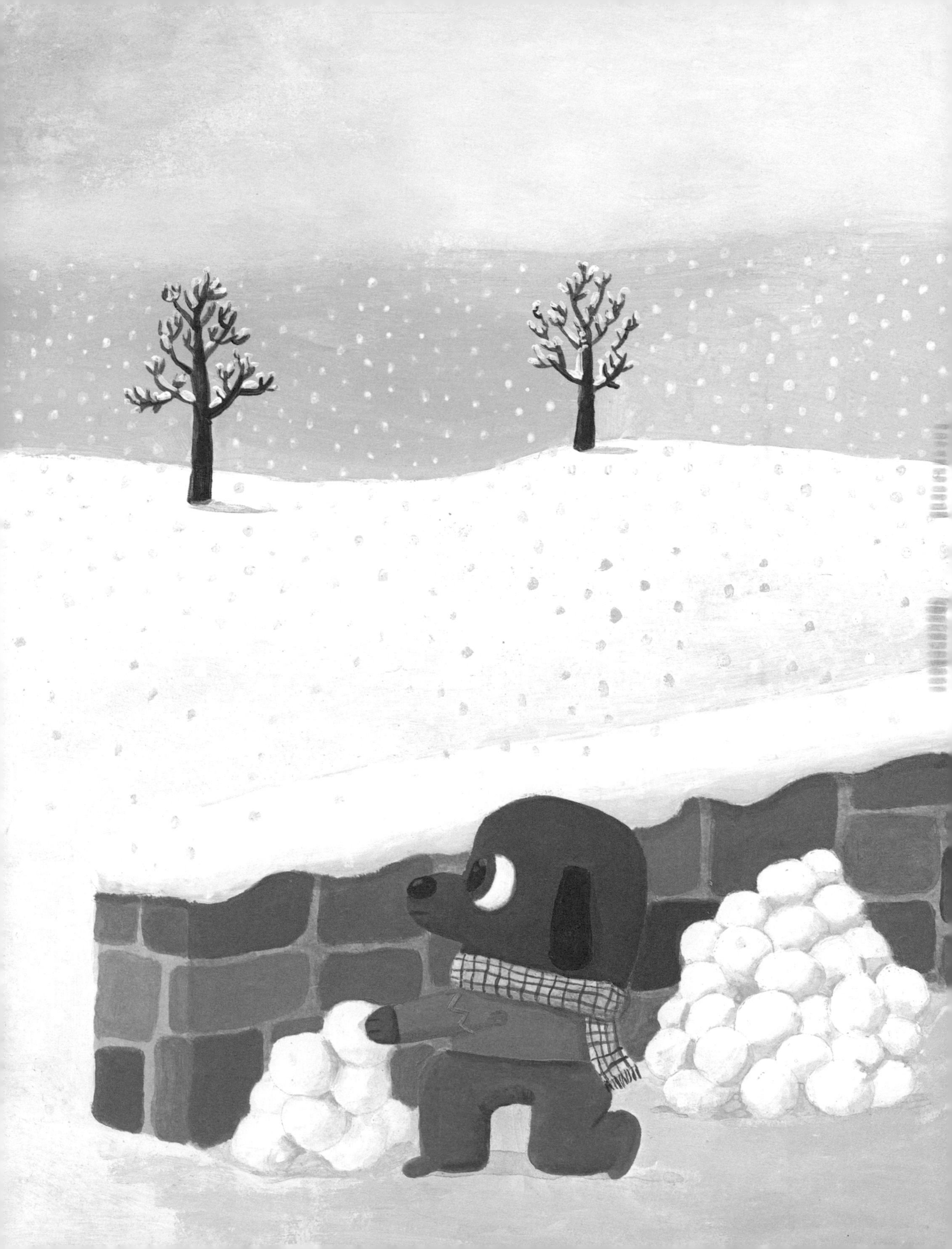

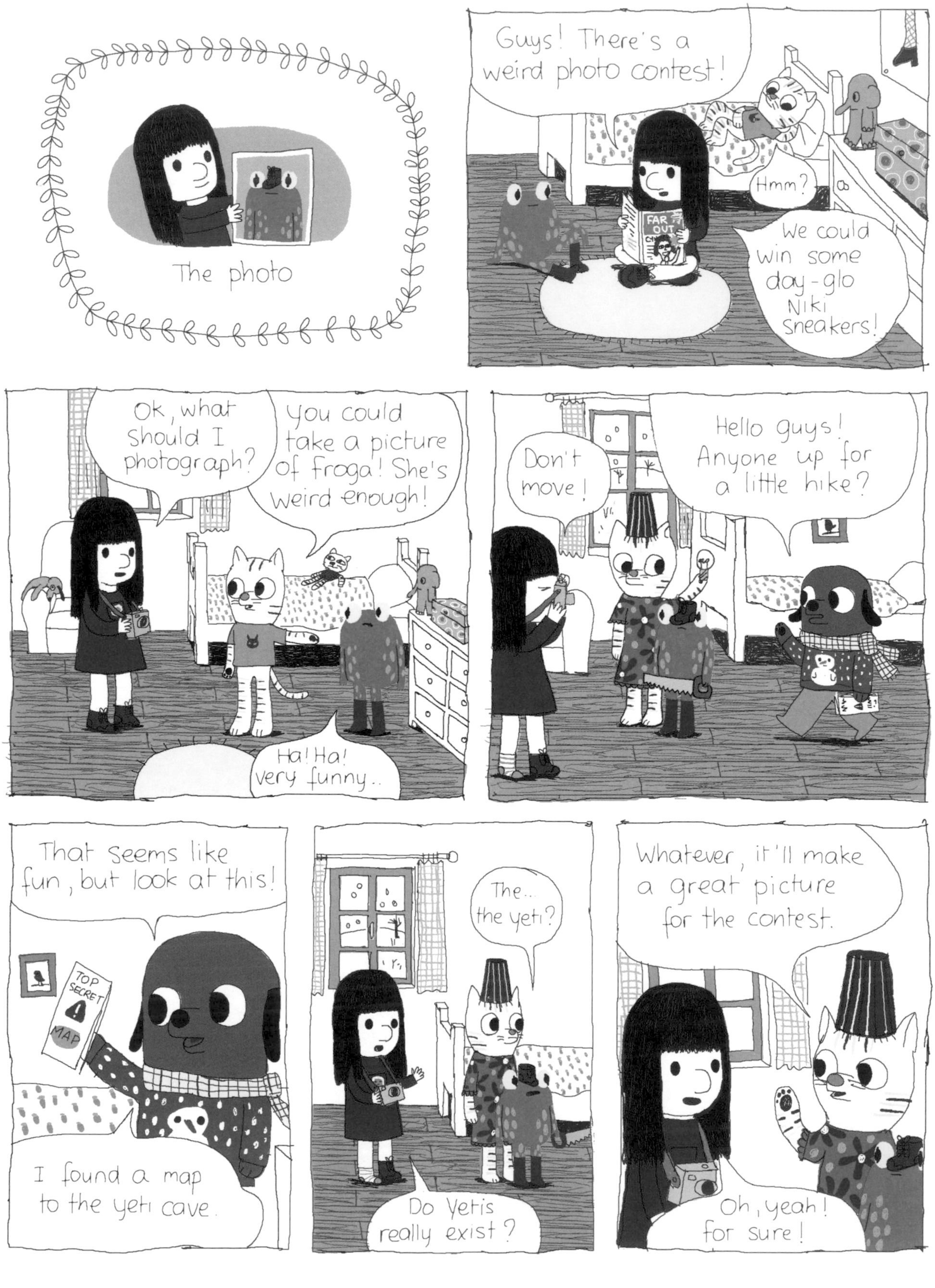
The photo
Guys! There's a weird photo contest!
Hmm?
We could win some day-glo Niki sneakers!
FAR OUT
Ok, what should I photograph?
You could take a picture of Froga! She's weird enough!
Ha! Ha! very funny..
Don't move!
Hello guys! Anyone up for a little hike?
That seems like fun, but look at this!
TOP SECRET
MAP
I found a map to the yeti cave.
The... the yeti?
Do Yetis really exist?
Whatever, it'll make a great picture for the contest.
Oh, yeah! for sure!

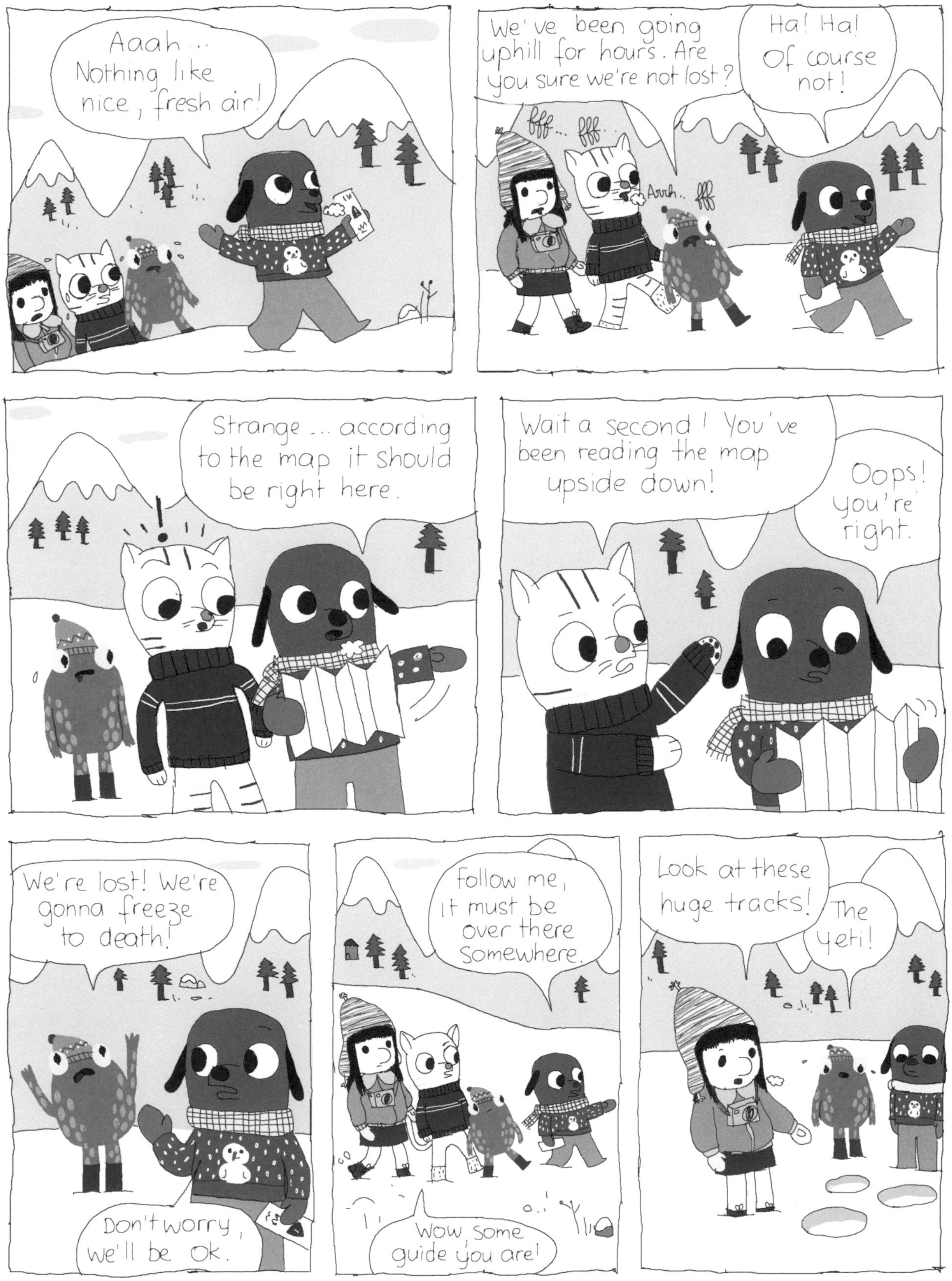
Aaah ... Nothing like nice, fresh air!
We've been going uphill for hours. Are you sure we're not lost?
Ha! Ha! Of course not!
fff... fff...
Arrh.. fff
Strange ... according to the map it should be right here.
Wait a second! You've been reading the map upside down!
Oops! You're right.
We're lost! We're gonna freeze to death!
Don't worry, we'll be Ok.
Follow me, it must be over there somewhere.
Wow, some guide you are!
Look at these huge tracks!
The Yeti!

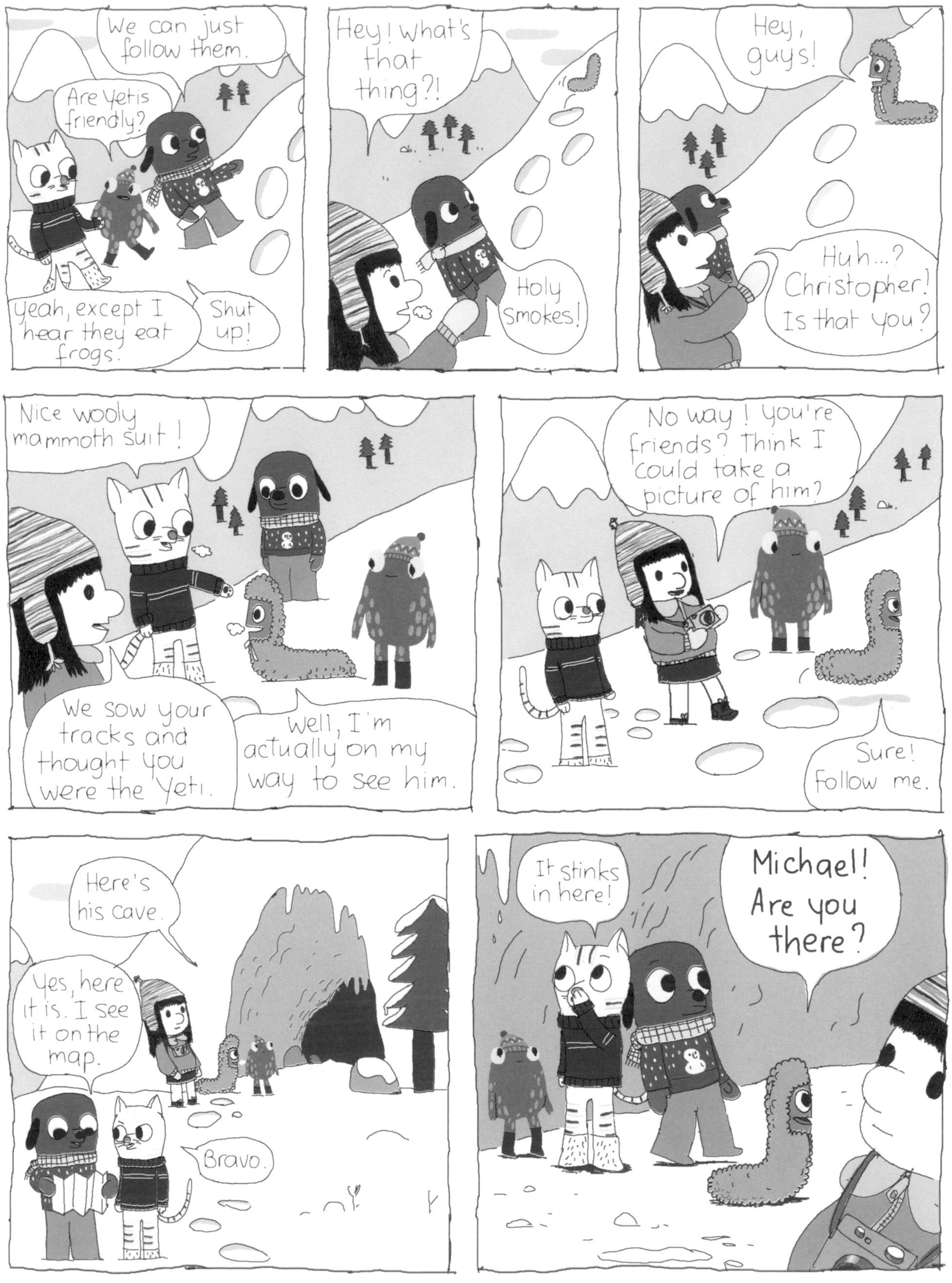

We can just follow them.
Are Yetis friendly?
Yeah, except I hear they eat frogs.
Shut up!
Hey! What's that thing?!
Holy smokes!
Hey, guys!
Huh...? Christopher! Is that you?
Nice wooly mammoth suit!
We sow your tracks and thought you were the Yeti.
Well, I'm actually on my way to see him.
No way! You're friends? Think I could take a picture of him?
Sure! Follow me.
Here's his cave.
Yes, here it is. I see it on the map.
Bravo.
It stinks in here!
Michael! Are you there?

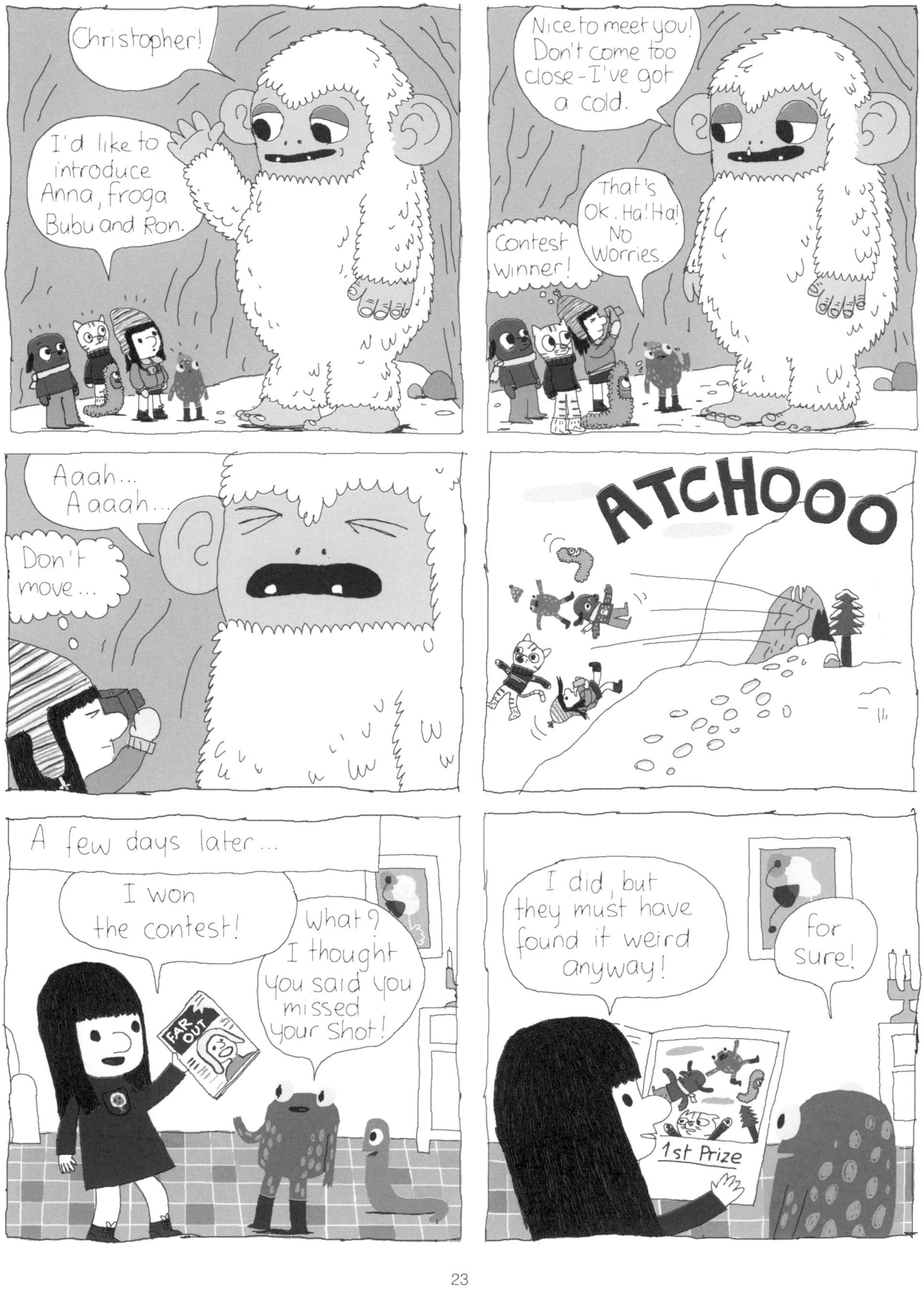

Christopher!
I'd like to introduce Anna, froga Bubu and Ron.
Nice to meet you! Don't come too close - I've got a cold.
Contest winner!
That's Ok. Ha! Ha! No Worries.
Aaah... Aaaah...
Don't move...
ATCHOOO
A few days later...
I won the contest!
What? I thought you said you missed your shot!
FAR OUT
I did, but they must have found it weird anyway!
for sure!
1st Prize

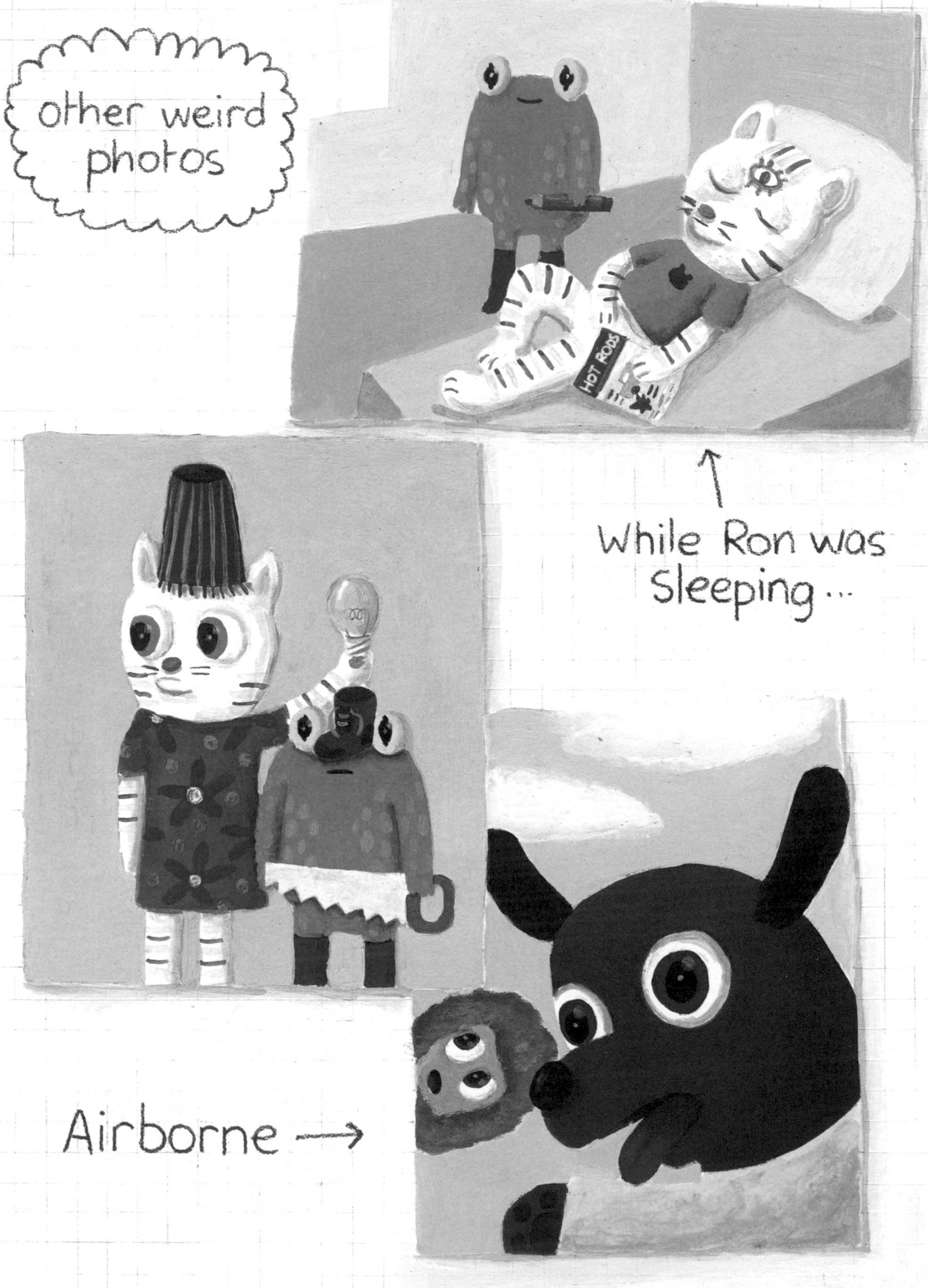
other weird photos
HOT RODS
While Ron was Sleeping...
Airborne →

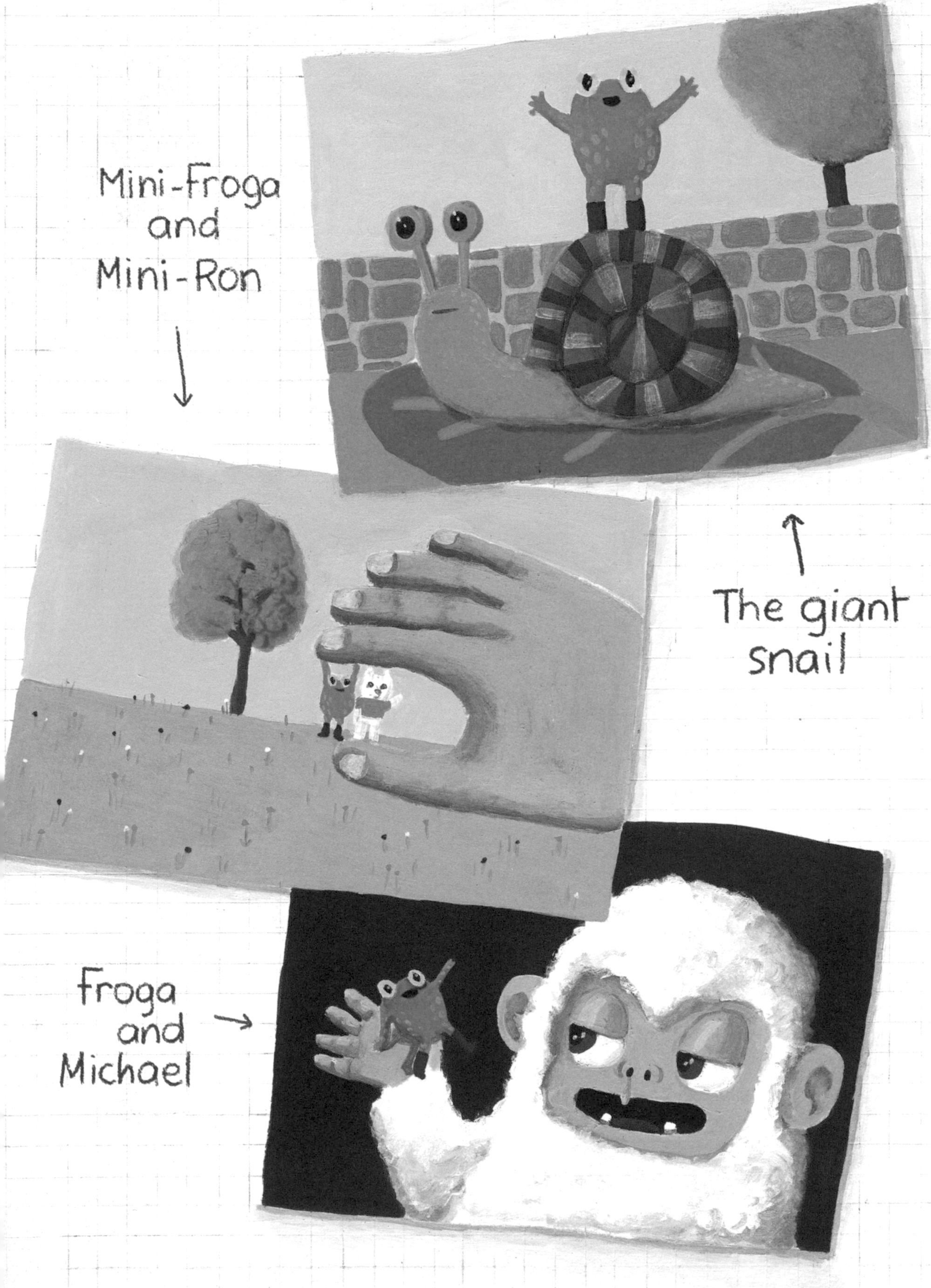

Mini-Froga and Mini-Ron
The giant snail
Froga and Michael

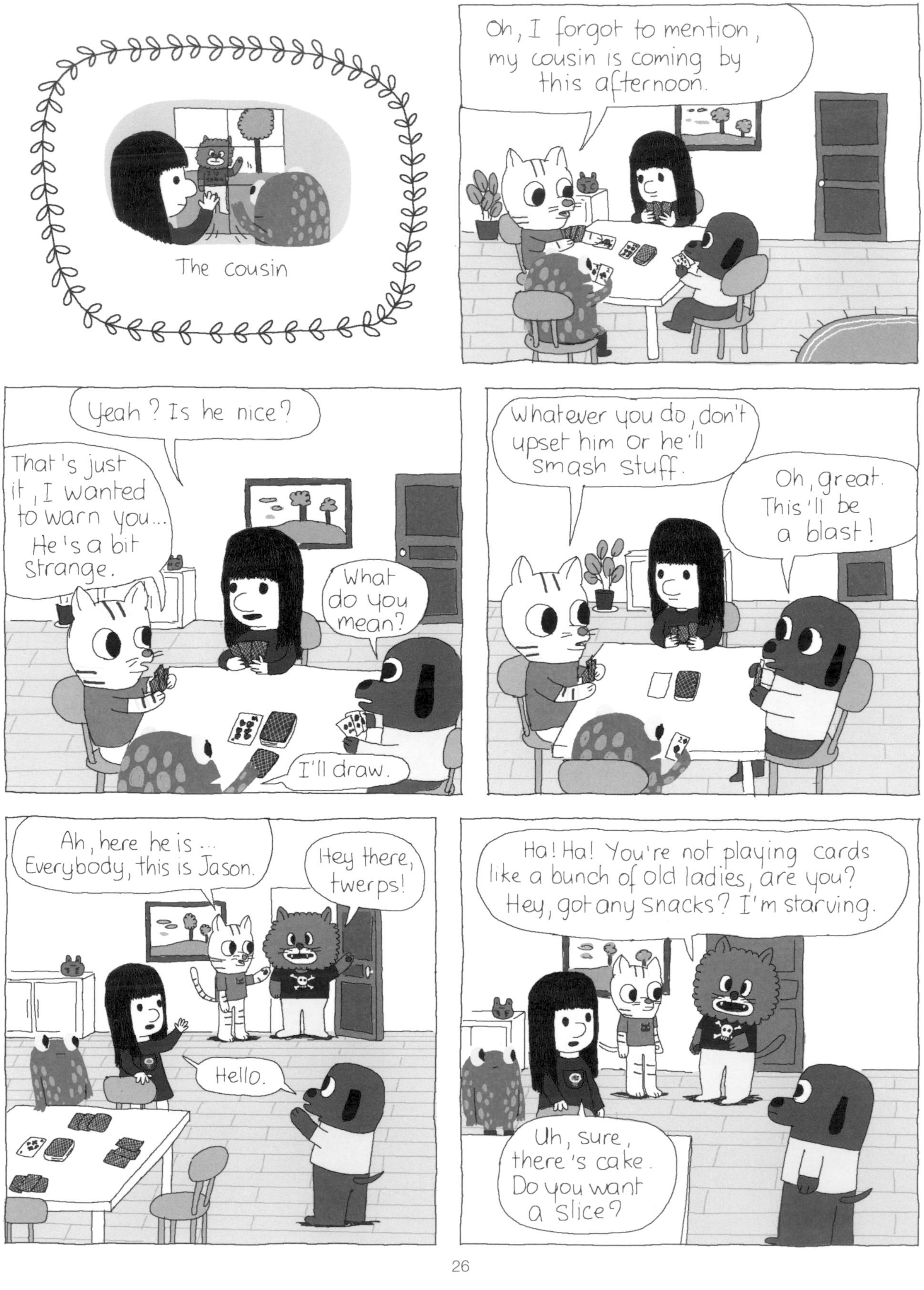
The cousin
Oh, I forgot to mention, my cousin is coming by this afternoon.
Yeah? Is he nice?
That's just it, I wanted to warn you... He's a bit strange.
What do you mean?
I'll draw.
Whatever you do, don't upset him or he'll smash stuff.
Oh, great. This'll be a blast!
Ah, here he is... Everybody, this is Jason.
Hey there, twerps!
Hello.
Ha! Ha! You're not playing cards like a bunch of old ladies, are you? Hey, got any snacks? I'm starving.
Uh, sure, there's cake. Do you want a slice?

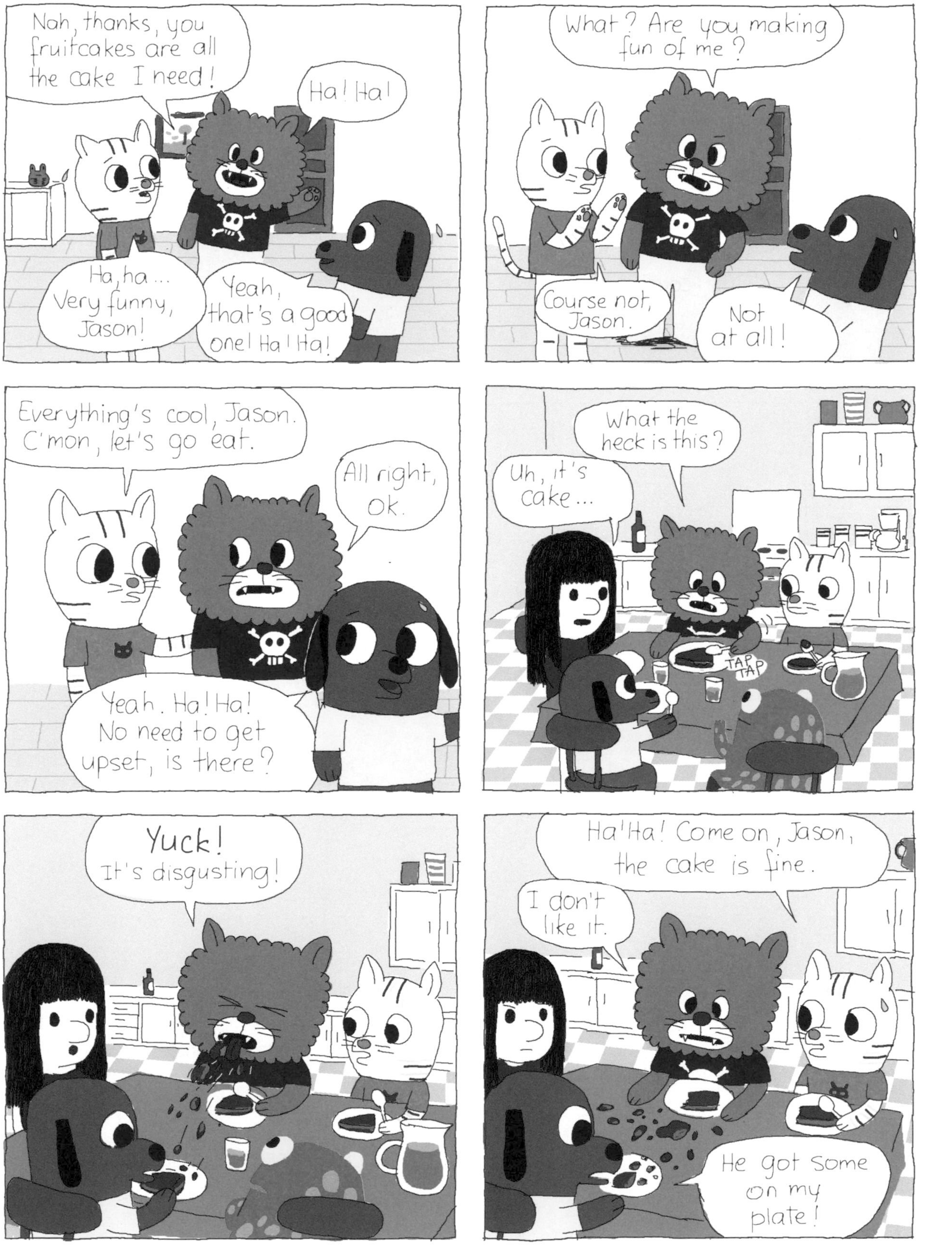
Nah, thanks, you fruitcakes are all the cake I need!
Ha! Ha!
Ha, ha... Very funny, Jason!
Yeah, that's a good one! Ha! Ha!
What? Are you making fun of me?
Course not, Jason.
Not at all!
Everything's cool, Jason. C'mon, let's go eat.
All right, ok.
Yeah. Ha! Ha! No need to get upset, is there?
Uh, it's cake...
What the heck is this?
TAP TAP
Yuck! It's disgusting!
I don't like it.
Ha! Ha! Come on, Jason, the cake is fine.
He got some on my plate!

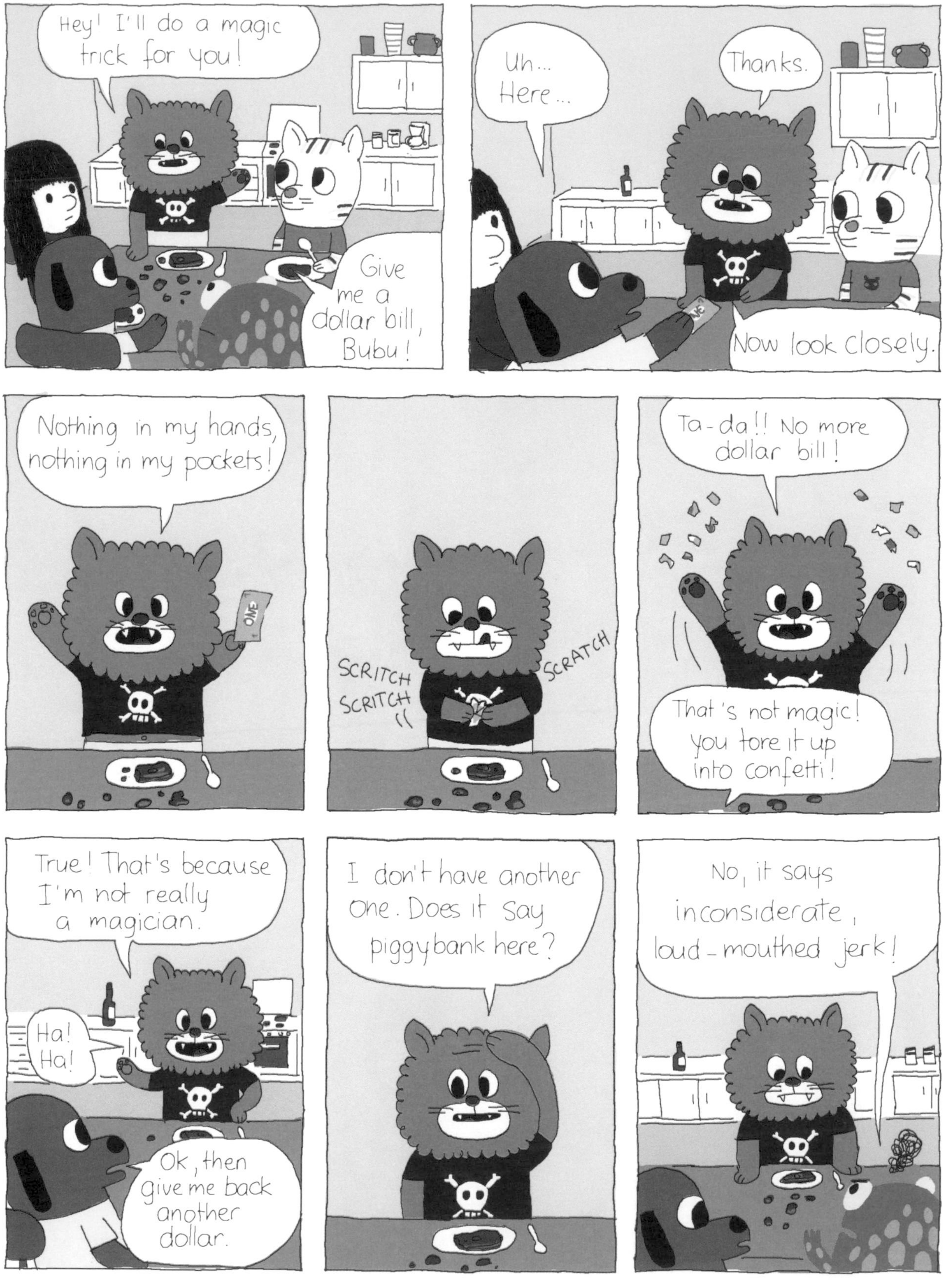
Hey! I'll do a magic trick for you!
Give me a dollar bill, Bubu!
Uh... Here...
Thanks.
Now look closely.
Nothing in my hands, nothing in my pockets!
ONE
SCRITCH SCRITCH
SCRATCH
Ta-da!! No more dollar bill!
That's not magic! you tore it up into confetti!
True! That's because I'm not really a magician.
Ha! Ha!
Ok, then give me back another dollar.
I don't have another one. Does it say piggybank here?
No, it says inconsiderate, loud-mouthed jerk!

Jerk ? She.. sniff .. called .. me .. a ... jerk ?
BOO HOO HOO
C'mon, it's all right!
Snirf!
Uh... I thought he smashes stuff!
I guess he's changed.
Great. And I've been biting my tongue so I wouldn't upset him.
I've got an idea! Ron will take you out for ice cream and you can spend the afternoon together.
Sure, I guess.
Boo hoo
Thanks, guys!
Anytime!
Sniff! Nobody likes me!
Ha! Ha! Fooled you! You didn't really think that bunch of knuckleheads could make me cry, did you? Now it's just you and me!
I've always wondered, where'd you get that ugly nose?
Ever consider plastic surgery?
Pfff
How far is it? I don't feel like walking forever.

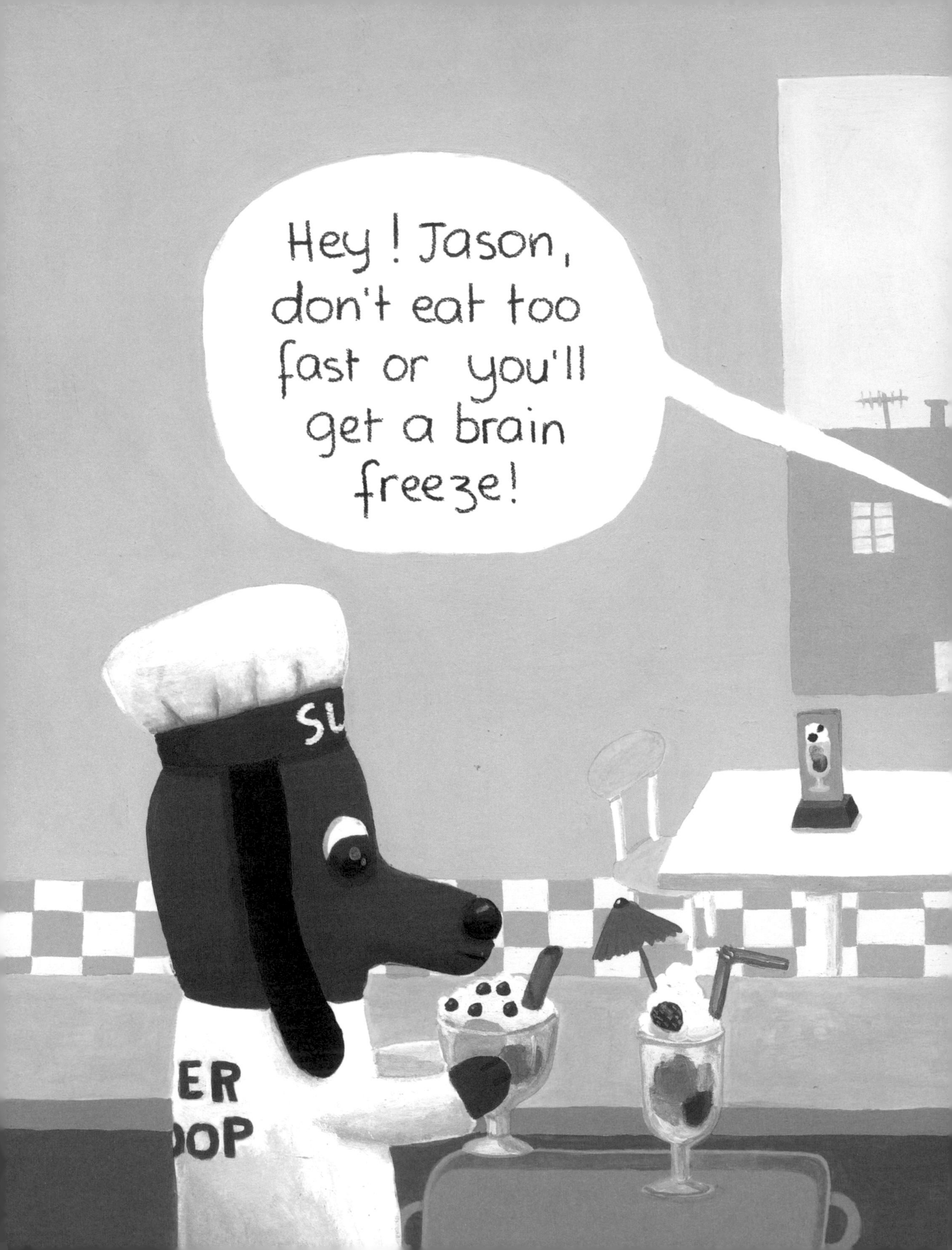
Hey! Jason, don't eat too fast or you'll get a brain freeze!
SU
ER
OOP

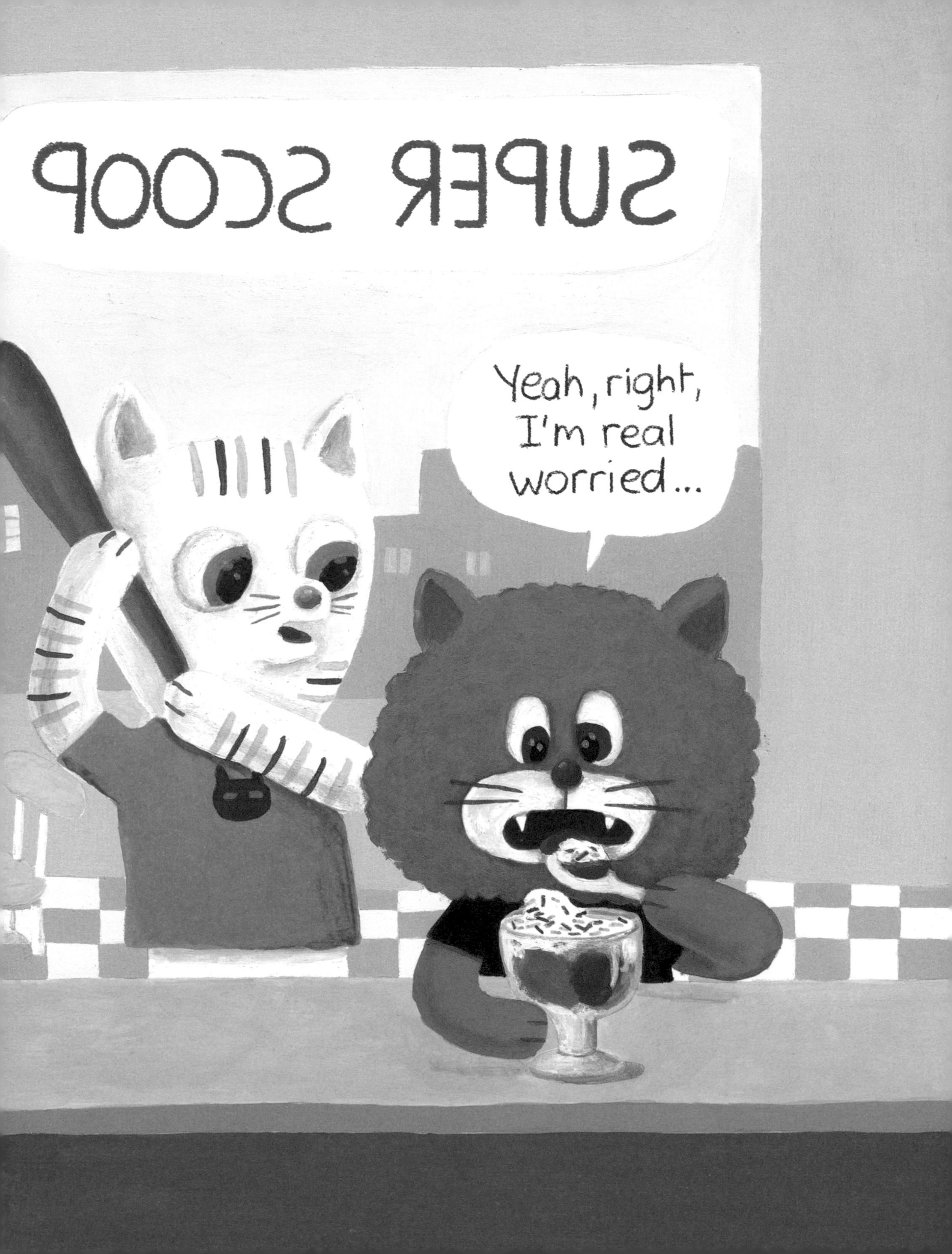
SUPER SCOOP
Yeah, right, I'm real worried...

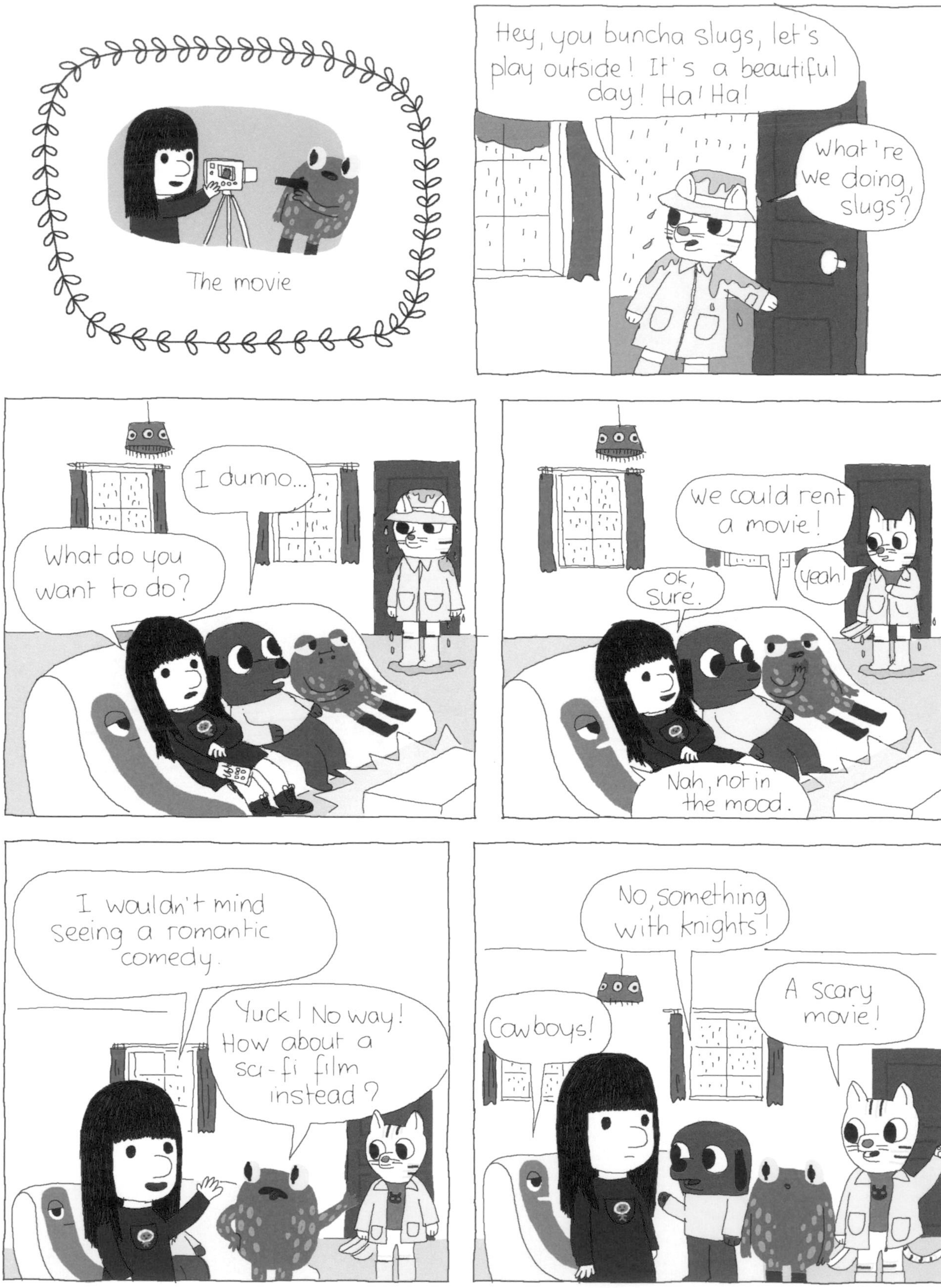
The movie
Hey, you buncha slugs, let's play outside! It's a beautiful day! Ha! Ha!
What're we doing, slugs?
I dunno...
What do you want to do?
We could rent a movie!
Ok, sure.
Yeah!
Nah, not in the mood.
I wouldn't mind seeing a romantic comedy.
Yuck! No way! How about a sci-fi film instead?
No, something with knights!
Cowboys!
A scary movie!

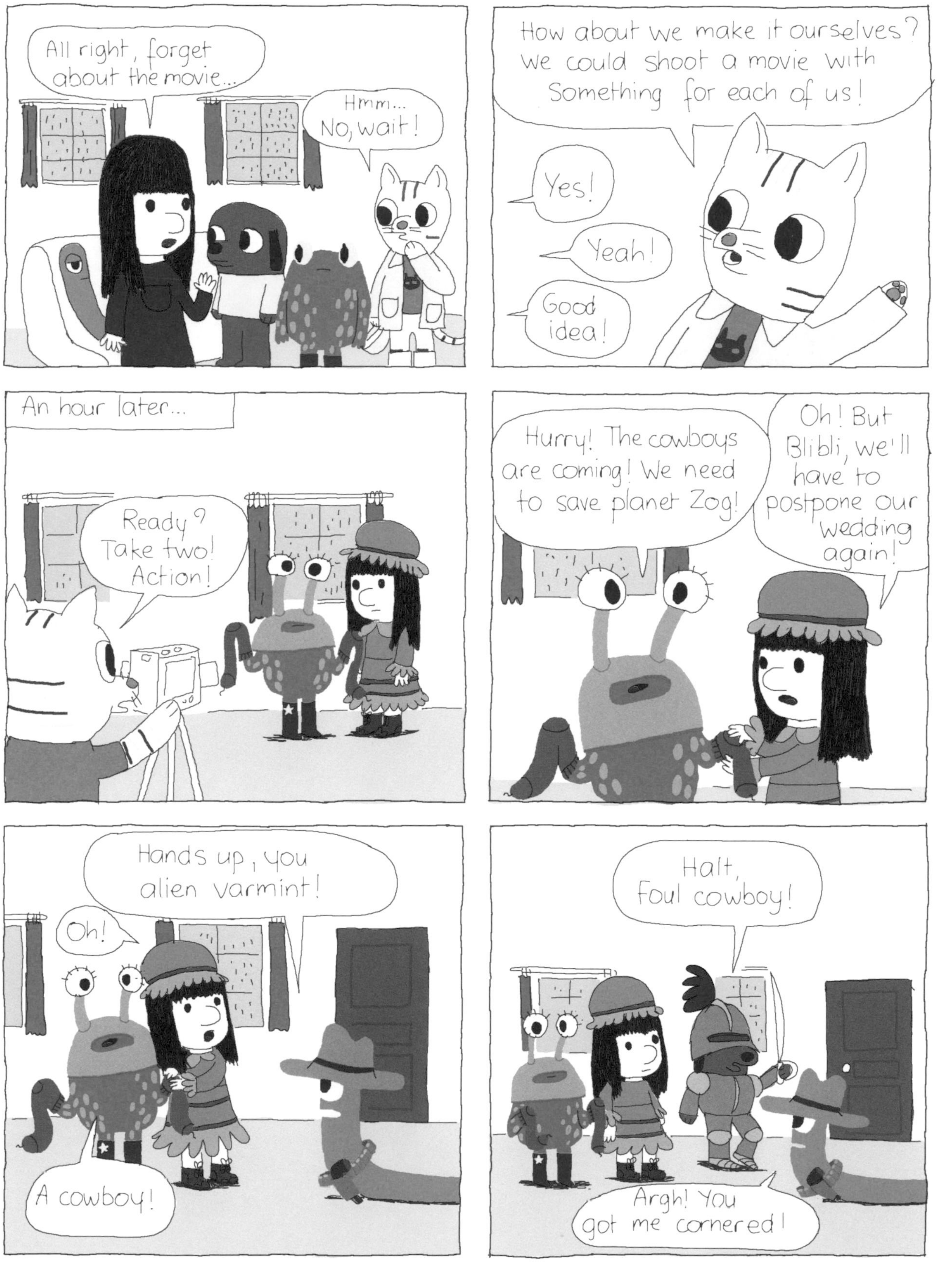
All right, forget about the movie...
Hmm... No, wait!
How about we make it ourselves? We could shoot a movie with Something for each of us!
Yes!
Yeah!
Good idea!
An hour later...
Ready? Take two! Action!
Hurry! The cowboys are coming! We need to save planet Zog!
Oh! But Blibli, we'll have to postpone our wedding again!
Hands up, you alien varmint!
Oh!
A cowboy!
Halt, Foul cowboy!
Argh! You got me cornered!

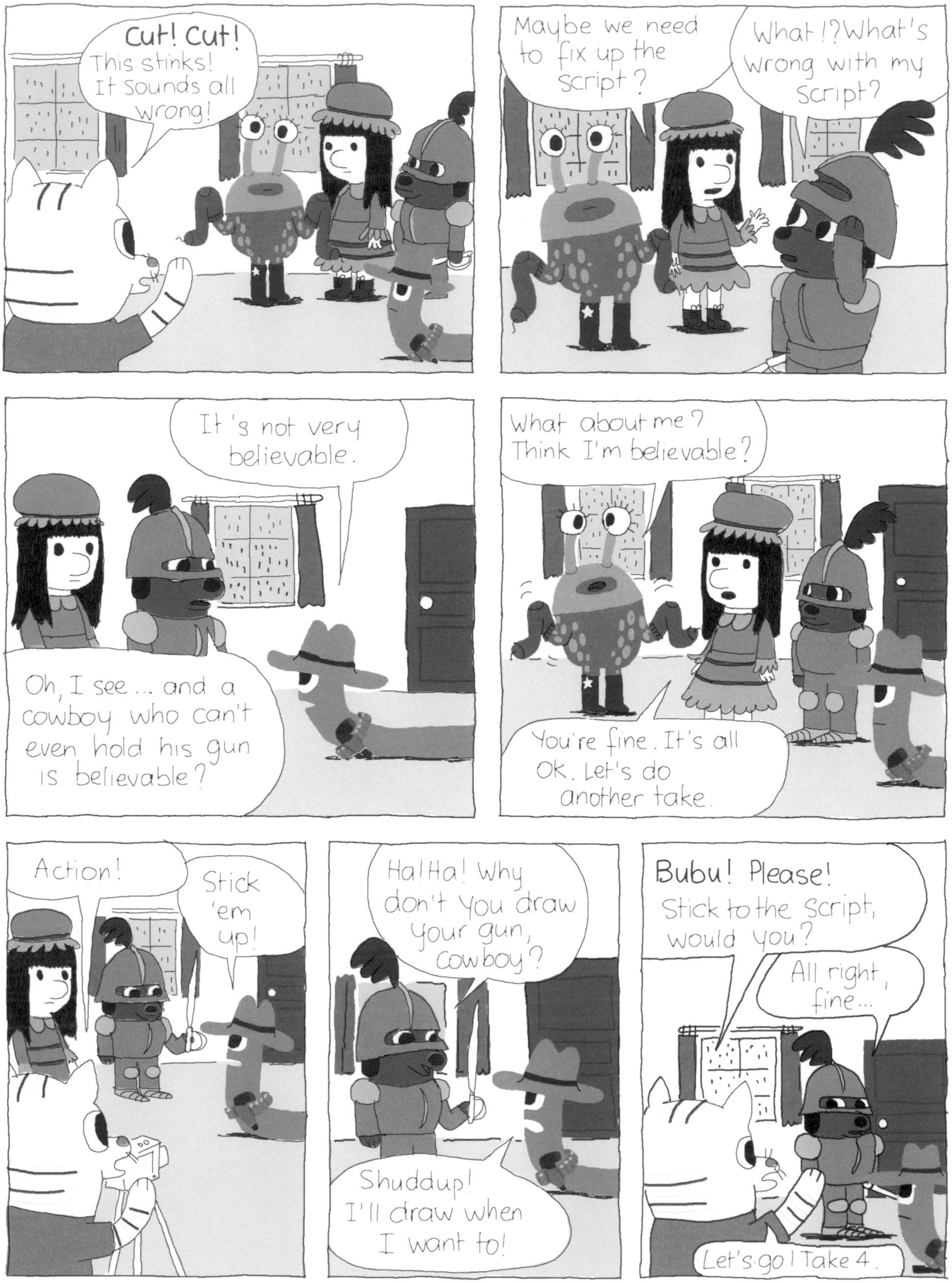
Cut! Cut! This stinks! It sounds all wrong!
Maybe we need to fix up the script?
What!? What's wrong with my script?
It's not very believable.
Oh, I see... and a cowboy who can't even hold his gun is believable?
What about me? Think I'm believable?
You're fine. It's all OK. Let's do another take.
Action!
Stick 'em up!
Ha! Ha! Why don't you draw your gun, cowboy?
Shuddup! I'll draw when I want to!
Bubu! Please! Stick to the script, would you?
All right, fine...
Let's go! Take 4.

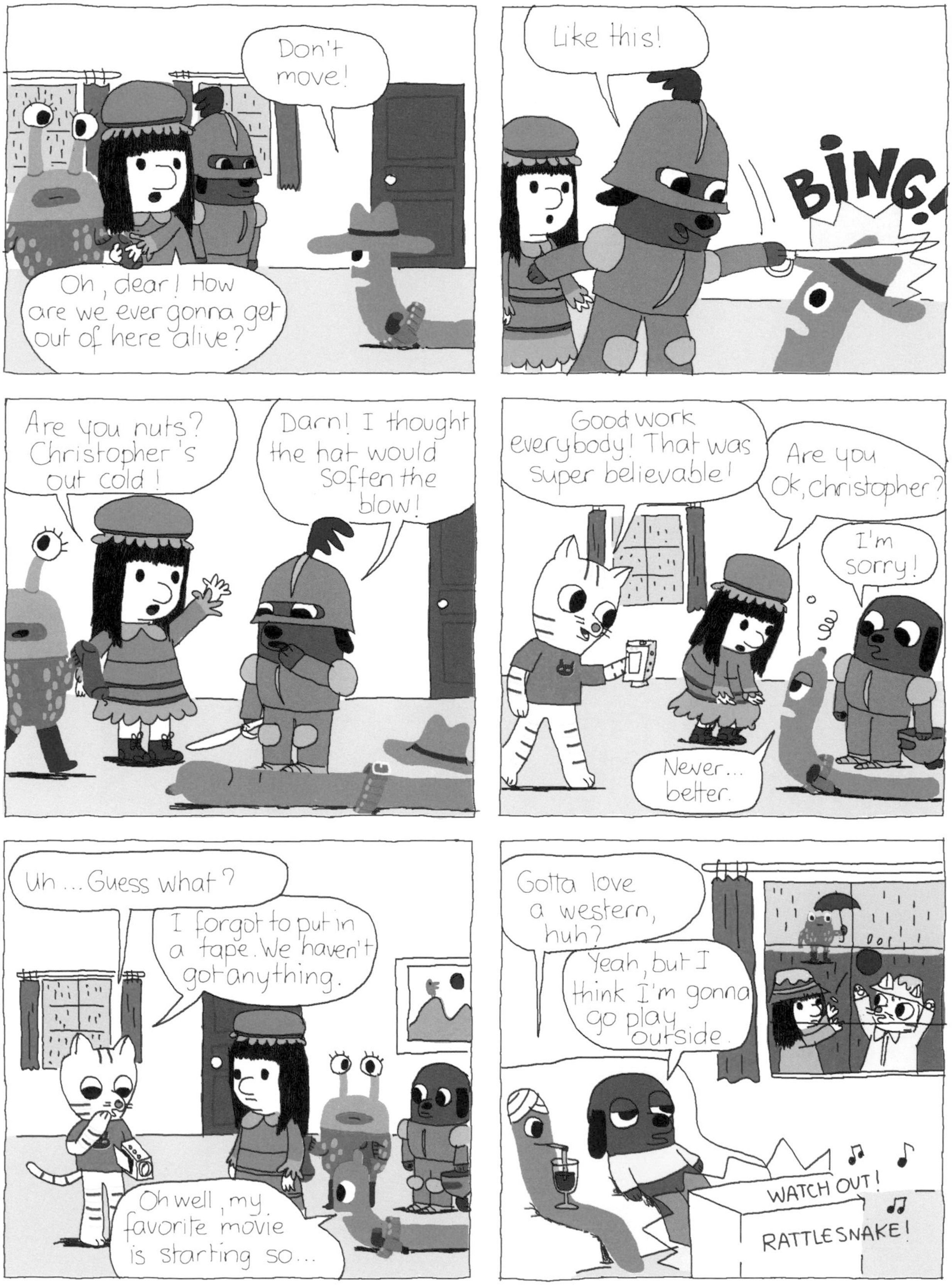
Don't move!
Oh, dear! How are we ever gonna get out of here alive?
Like this!
BING!
Are you nuts? Christopher's out cold!
Darn! I thought the hat would soften the blow!
Good work everybody! That was super believable!
Are you Ok, Christopher?
I'm sorry!
Never... better.
Uh... Guess what?
I forgot to put in a tape. We haven't got anything.
Oh well, my favorite movie is starting so...
Gotta love a western, huh?
Yeah, but I think I'm gonna go play outside.
WATCH OUT!
RATTLESNAKE!

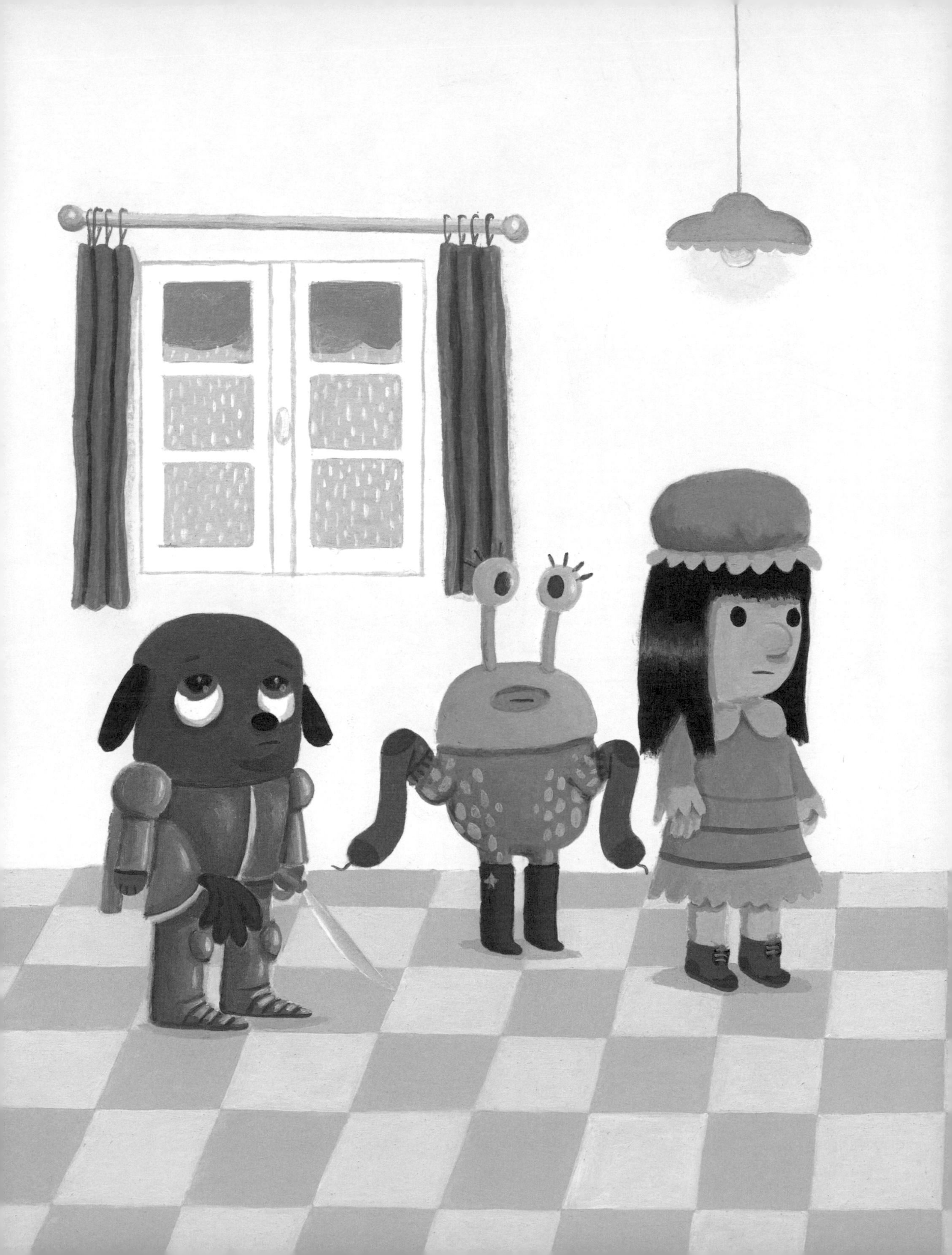

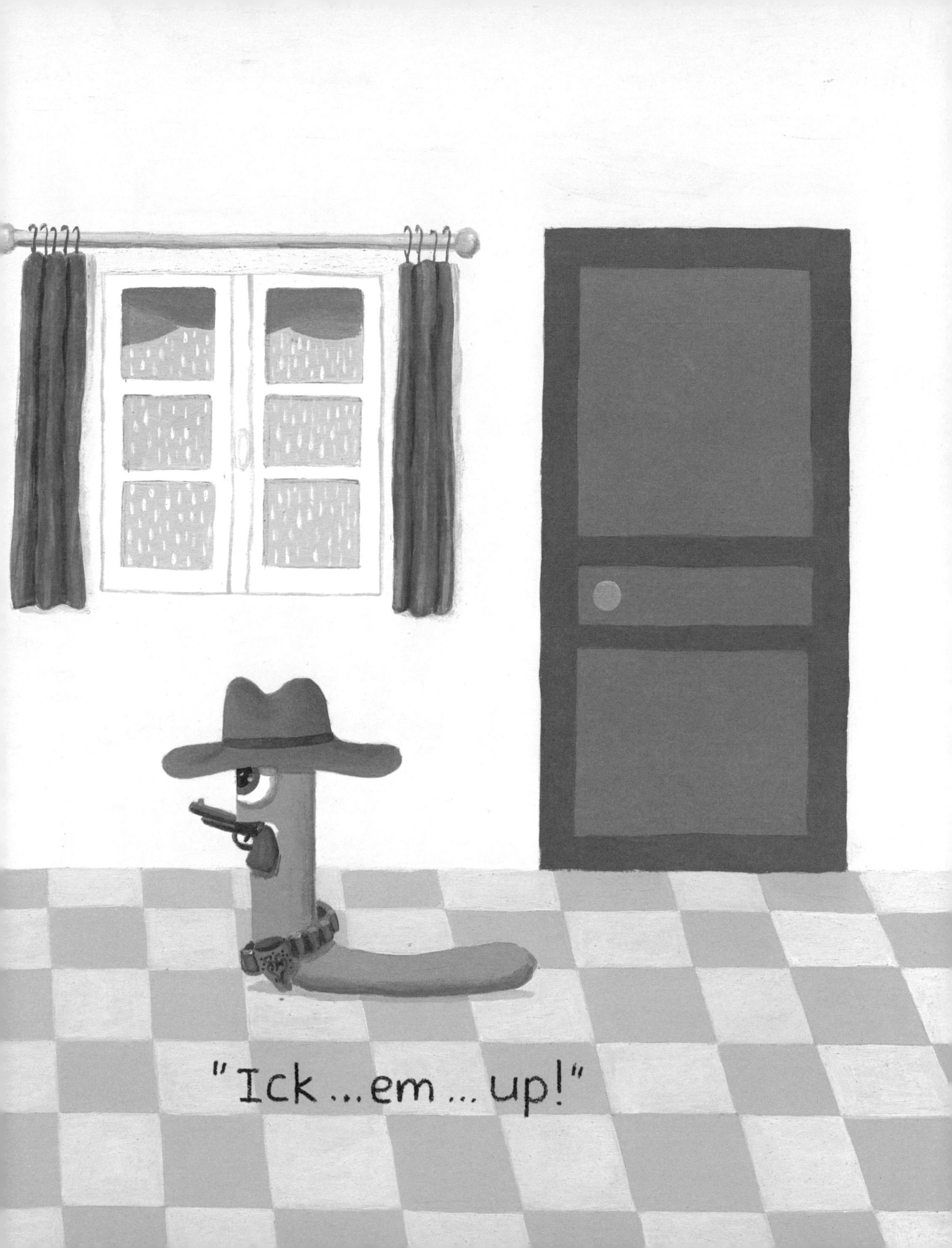

"Ick ... em ... up!"

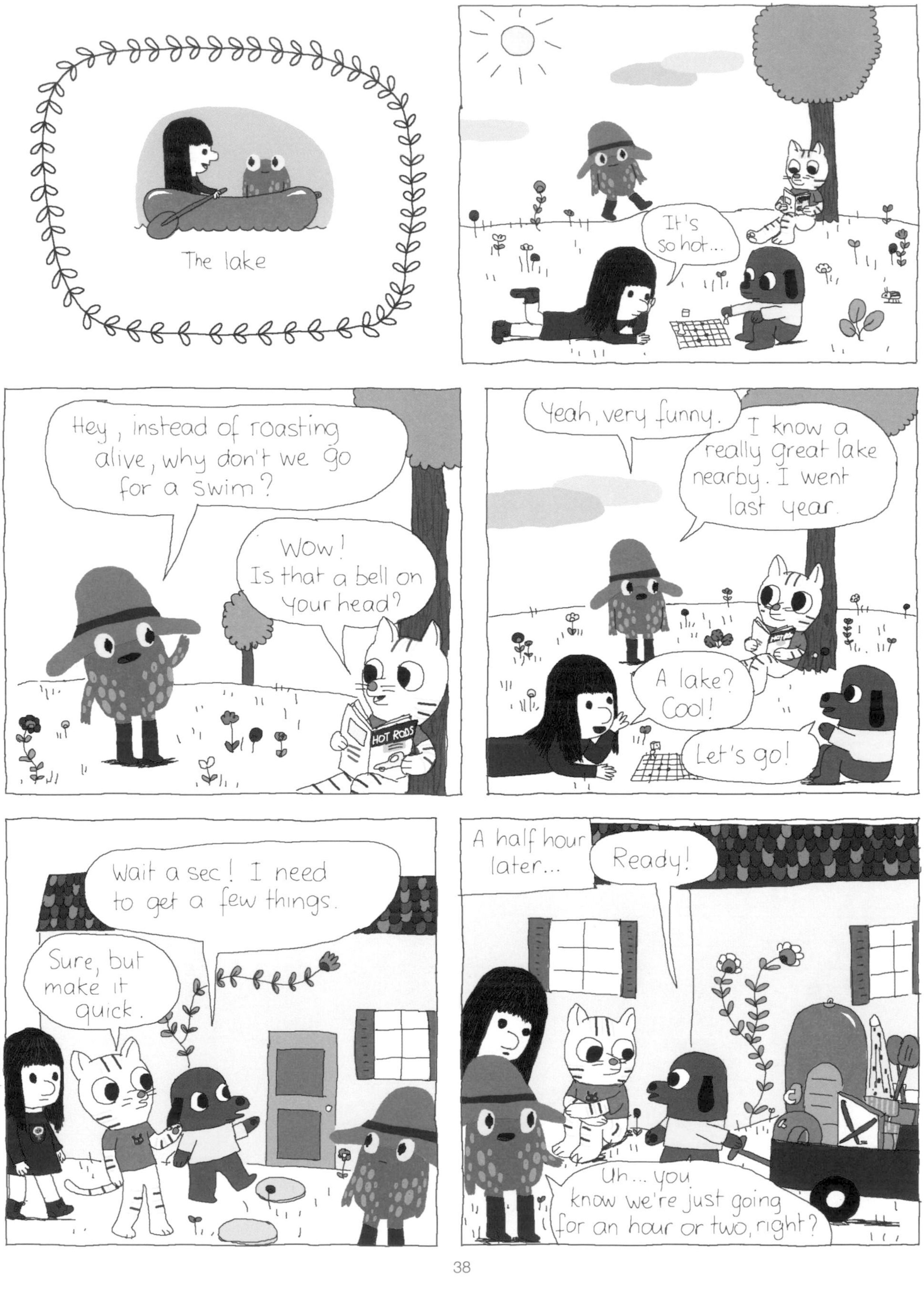
The lake
It's so hot...
Hey, instead of roasting alive, why don't we go for a swim?
Wow! Is that a bell on your head?
HOT RODS
Yeah, very funny.
I know a really great lake nearby. I went last year.
A lake? Cool!
Let's go!
Wait a sec! I need to get a few things.
Sure, but make it quick.
A half hour later...
Ready!
Uh... you know we're just going for an hour or two, right?

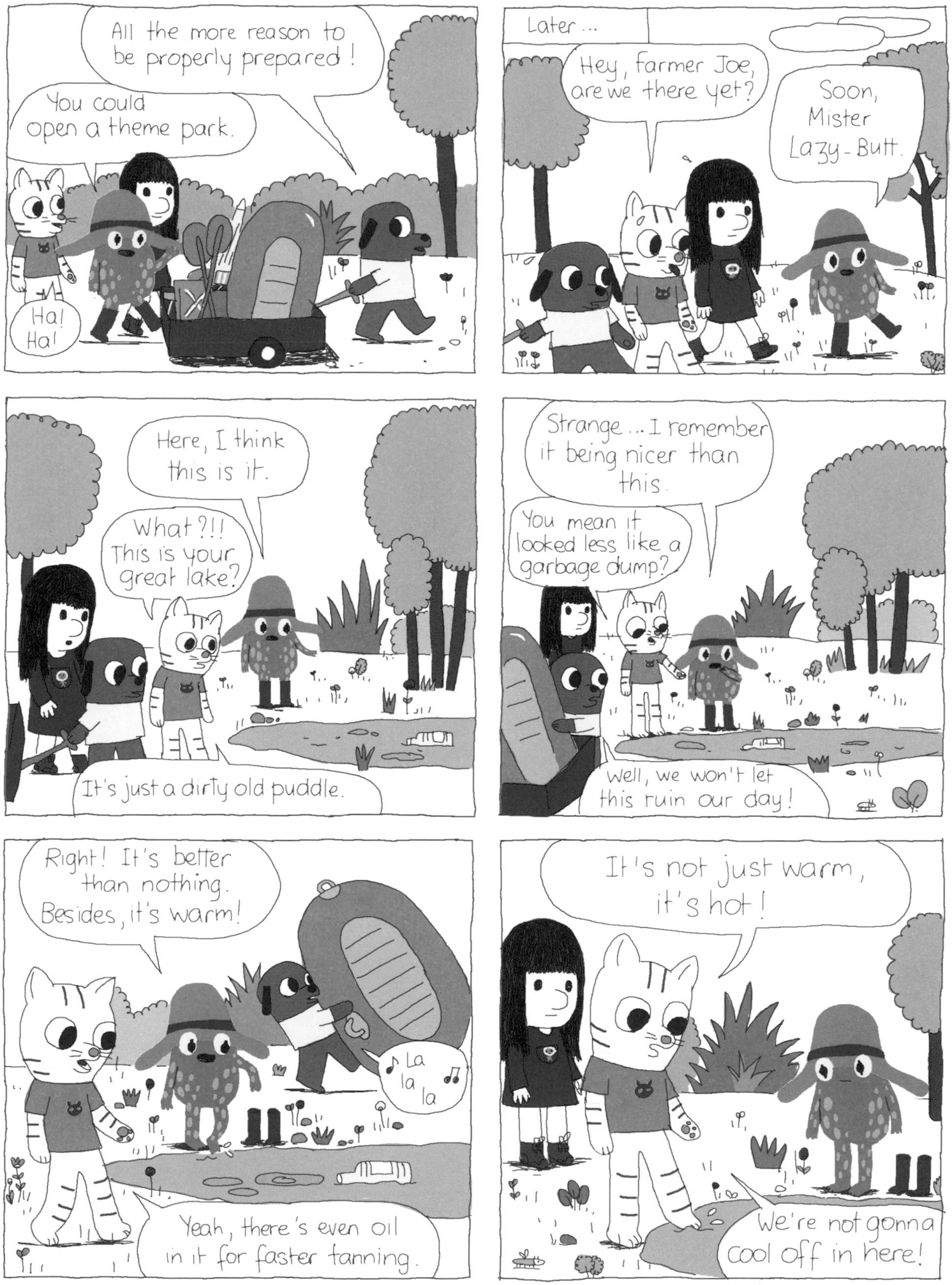
All the more reason to be properly prepared!
You could open a theme park.
Ha! Ha!
Later...
Hey, farmer Joe, are we there yet?
Soon, Mister Lazy-Butt.
Here, I think this is it.
What?!!! This is your great lake?
It's just a dirty old puddle.
Strange... I remember it being nicer than this.
You mean it looked less like a garbage dump?
Well, we won't let this ruin our day!
Right! It's better than nothing. Besides, it's warm!
♪ La la la ♫
Yeah, there's even oil in it for faster tanning.
It's not just warm, it's hot!
We're not gonna cool off in here!

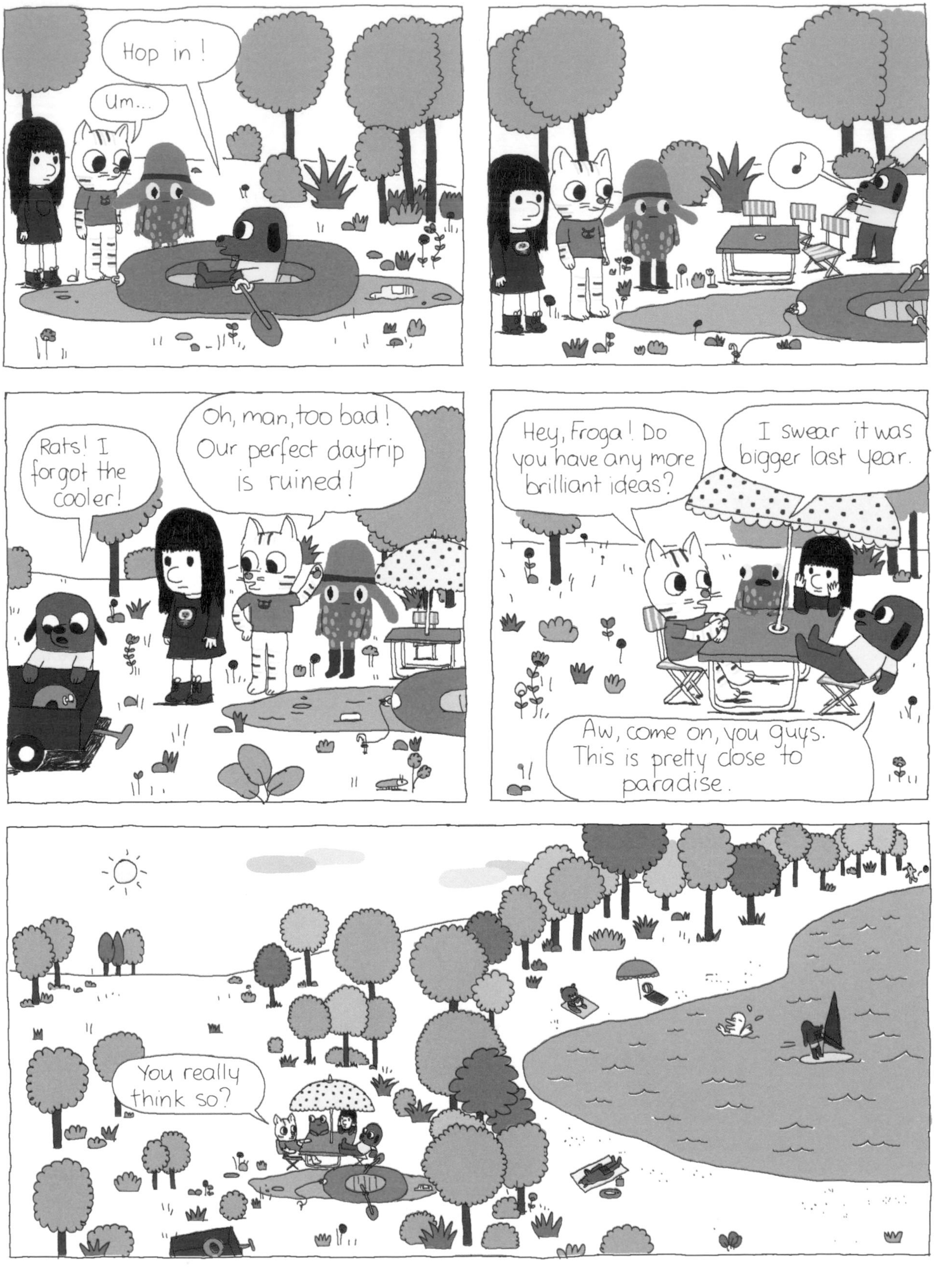
Hop in!
Um...
Rats! I forgot the cooler!
Oh, man, too bad! Our perfect daytrip is ruined!
Hey, Froga! Do you have any more brilliant ideas?
I swear it was bigger last year.
Aw, come on, you guys. This is pretty close to paradise.
You really think so?

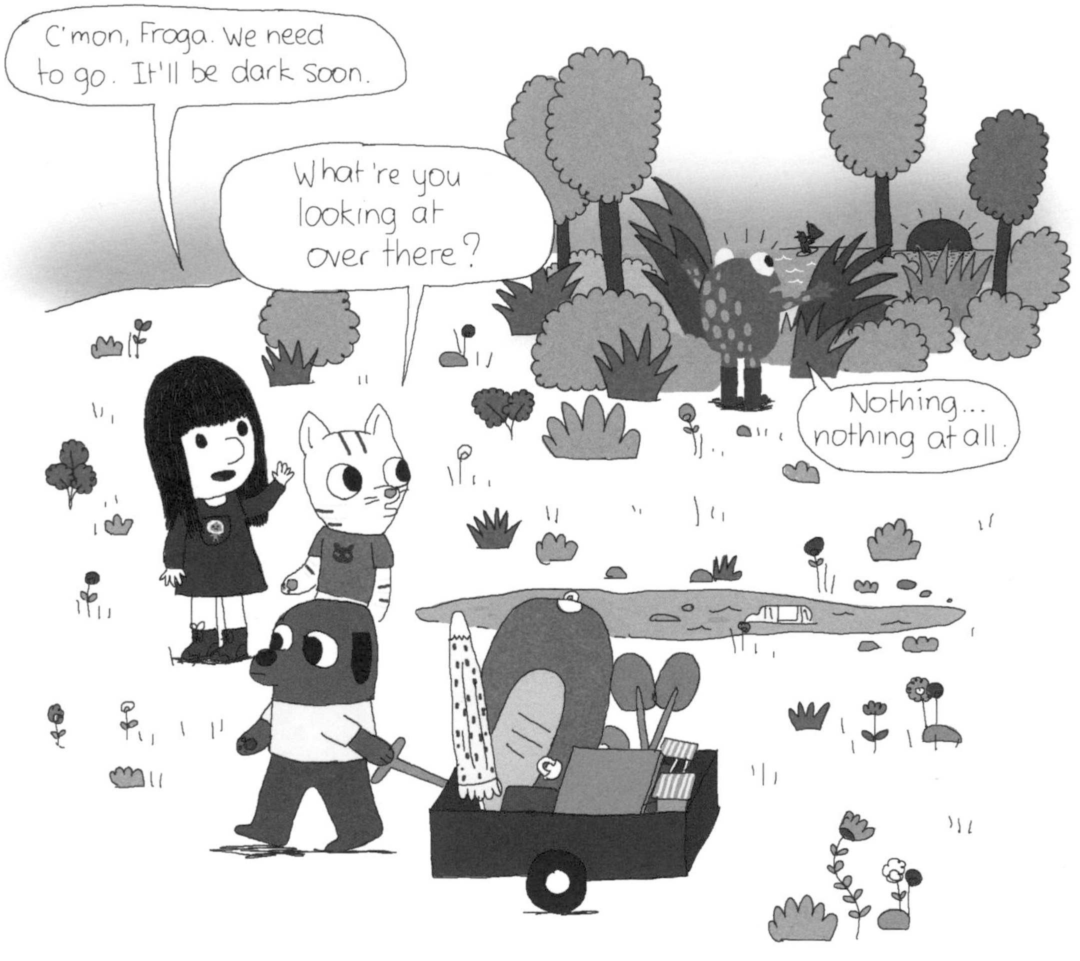
C'mon, Froga. We need to go. It'll be dark soon.
What're you looking at over there?
Nothing... nothing at all.

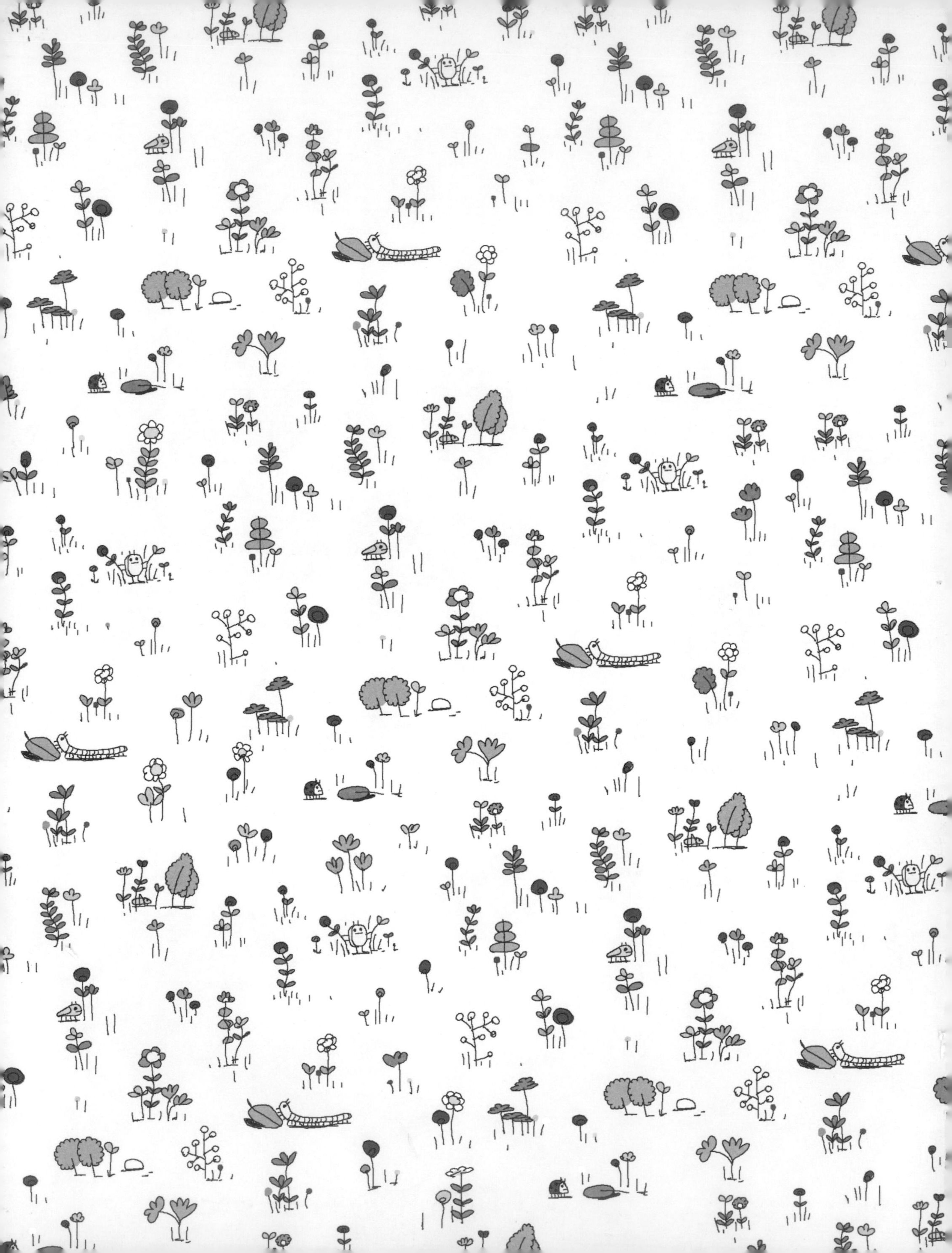